fly

By Erica Monzingo

fly

For Jen Loya, who knew I was a writer before I ever did.

prologue

Hiccups.

They're a tell-tale sign, a built-in warning of sorts, that my sleeping pills have begun to kick in full strength. I pull back my long brown curls and bind them into a pony tail and watch my eyes widen in the mirror at every unexpected hiccup. I scurry to gather the items needed to wash my face before I become delusional and forget what washing my face even is. I'm fully aware that – thanks to my sleeping pill – the next stage after hiccups is complete disorientation and the inability to stand up straight. There have been plenty of nights that I've ended up crawling the short distance from my bathroom to my bedroom in order to prevent bumps and bruises caused by falling against the walls. I methodically rub my cleansing cloth together to lather it up and start rubbing the makeup from my eyes. I sneak quick gasps of air through my mouth in order to prevent myself from inhaling the soap through my nose. After splashing my face with water a few times, I blindly grab for the purple face towel hanging on the back of the bathroom door and begin to pat my skin dry.

"You still have bubbles in your hairline," a male voice says from beside me. I jump and my eyes fly open, wide with fear.

"Kellen! What did I tell you about sneaking up on me?!" I shriek as I throw the towel at him in an effort to calm my now-shaken nerves. He brings the towel to his face so I can only see his blonde spiky hair and snickers into it. "It's NOT funny," I scold as I rip the towel back out of his hands, hang it on the towel bar, and storm out of the bathroom.

To any other person, a small startle would have been no big deal. Any other person would have been able to recognize there was no real danger and go back to feeling perfectly normal. I, on the other hand, was in full-stealth mode, ready to either take off in a full-on sprint down the hall towards safety or prepare for the fight of my life. While everyone else has a functioning "fear center," mine was a bit overactive and currently making my entire body hum from confusion about why I wasn't running away.

I'm still shaking from the startle of his sudden appearance as I peel back the covers to my bed and start to arrange my pillows into a makeshift fort. The more concealed and hidden I feel from the rest of the world while I sleep, the more likely I'll actually be able to stay asleep.

fly

"Amelia ..." I hear Kellen call for me down the hall. His slow approach is probably in part because he knows he's made me mad and in part because he wants to warn me so I don't mistake him for a stranger walking through my doorway and punch him square in the face. I glance up to see him leaning against my door frame, and I shoot him an "I'm pissed off leave me alone" look before disappearing into my fortress of pillows.

"There's a body pillow taking up my spot in there," he says softly as he inches closer to the bed. I let out a disgruntled, "Yeah, so?" and bury myself deeper into the covers.

"Millie, I'm really sorry. I'll start loudly announcing my arrival from now on ... from very far away so you have plenty of time to realize I'm here."

I hear his muffled voice through the layers of blankets covering me. I poke my head out to scold him for knowing better than to sneak up on me like that, especially considering how my brain works, but I see the sullen expression on his face and realize he actually fears I won't let him in my bed. He's crouched to my level, and his eyes are wide enough for me to take notice of every tiny speck of green they hold. I stare at him for a minute, taking note of every curve along his jawline and the rise and fall of his cheekbones, every dimple, the way his hair falls. I need these memories, for the day and time when I can't see him at all.

Turning away from him and kick the body pillow off of the bed and pull back the covers. He makes his way to the opposite

7

side of my bed and climbs in, sitting with his back against the wall. I prop myself up on my left elbow, waiting for him to settle before I nestle in beside him. I press the front of my body as hard as I can against his right side, slipping my leg over his to ensure there isn't an ounce of space between us. He drapes his right arm around my midsection, holding me closely, and I weave my left hand out from under me and across my stomach, winding my fingers through his. The hum of panic that was coursing through my body begins to subside, and I take a deep breath, allowing myself to melt against the comfort and familiarity of his body.

"Kellen?" I ask in a nearly inaudible, sleepy mumble. He gently swipes a strand of hair from my face in response. My body starts to softly tremble as tears fall down my face. My emotions are always tenfold after the pills have set in.

I keep my eyes closed tightly and my ear up against his chest, the beating of his heart the only sound I dare take in. With each thump my body starts to relax, muscles losing tension beat by beat until I melt into nothing. I can no longer remember the hell that was the hours before this moment or every exhausting minute of the day.

Nothing else exists.

I can feel his body against mine. I know every curve, every divot. I can feel the rise and fall of every muscle without even touching them. I absentmindedly slip my hand to his face and cradle the line of his jaw in my palm, gently rubbing his whiskers and then finding my way back to his hairline and feeling the softness of his hair pour between my fingers.

"I memorized you," I barely whisper, my hands now softly gliding down his arms and winding themselves through his soft hands. His breath pours over my head, coating me, putting me in a trance. The combination of spearmint gum and the deep, rich smell of his cologne fills the air around me becoming the only thing I can breathe in. He *was* my air.

Suddenly, my stomach turns and my lungs refuse to fill with air. Falling asleep curled up next to Kellen is a sharp stab in the chest reminder of the night I first saw him in my post pill hours and in the dreams that followed.

Forty-eight hours after he died.

chapter one
three months earlier

I met Kellen my junior year of high school. I had just transferred and started a new school year in a new town to escape problems I had at my old school. No one knew me, no one knew my secrets, and I was glad to get lost in a sea of people I didn't know. The plan was simple: don't talk to anyone, don't make a sound.

During classes I faced forward and didn't talk to the people around me. If they asked me a question, I answered, but for the most part, I kept to myself. My plan was to be as uninvolved in people's lives as I could manage because becoming overly involved in other people's lives is what had ultimately forced me to change schools in the first place. My plan, in all its simple glory, would have worked brilliantly, had there not been an unforeseeable force working against me.

During my second-hour study-hall, a boy named Corbin sat across from me and started conversation as though we were old friends. Corbin would walk with me between classes as well, and we'd always be joined by others. No matter how much I tried not to talk to anyone, they all acted like I was an essential part of any conversation. The same applied to lunch; I started out alone but was quickly surrounded by a certain group of people who chatted in the same fashion - rapidly and as if the conversation couldn't thrive without me. I wasn't sure what it was that I had to do in order to keep people at bay and far, far away from me. On the other hand, it didn't hurt to blend in.

Classes were a little different. There I could stay anonymous and to myself since I made a point of sitting in the front of the room. I made it through every class with the exception of one: sociology. In sociology, I had made it into class in time to get the front seat, but that seat was directly in front Kellen and his best friend, Anthony. They both found extreme entertainment in having me sit in front of them, no matter how much I ignored their existence. They were constantly talking to each other and then poking me in the back until I'd turn around and say, "Yes?" or eventually "What?!" And then they'd continue with their banter. They'd talk to each other and make sure I was included in their conversation. Kellen would ask Anthony something, and Anthony would with respond with, "I don't know; let's ask Amelia," as if I had been their third vote for their entire lives.

During lunch I sat with a group of juniors who had taken me under their collective wing. I noticed that Kellen and Anthony sat a few tables away with a few of their friends. I could see them from the corner of my eye, and they always looked so happy and careless.

"That's where everyone wants to be," a girl would whisper as she caught me glancing over at them. I turned to her with a confused look on my face, reluctant to start any conversation she'd mistake as friendship. "They're like, the most popular boys in school," she replied dreamily. I nodded and then rolled my eyes when I turned my head away from her. If only high schoolers could realize the importance of being able to treat everyone as an equal. A human was a human; no one was any better than other people.

The banter and jokes from Kellen and Anthony continued in my sociology class, and of course when the teacher said, "Get a group of three for the next project," I had sat silently as everyone else scurried to find their group. They were all afraid to be left out; I feared being included.

When she'd take note of every three-person group she'd say, "Did I miss anyone?" and I'd raise my hand and reply, "It's not a big deal, I don't mind doing it alone." Then she'd shrug because she wouldn't want to figure out where to put me or how to make a four-person group be fair.

That was my plan. But I was beginning to realize that any time I made a plan, the exact opposite thing happened. When the teacher called out Kellen's name, he let her know that Anthony and I were his partners and we'd be doing our report on "balls." The teacher rolled her eyes, but Anthony argued that "there are many types of balls ... golf balls, soccer balls, baseballs ..." I just shook my head and bowed it a bit. Wonderful.

As I walked out of the classroom, I heard Kellen yell after me, but I pretended as though I either hadn't heard him or hadn't realized that he was talking to me. "Millie!" he yelled out, but I didn't pay any attention to it. However, when I reached my locker, I realized I was at a dead end. He sprinted a little to catch up to me and placed his hand on my shoulder to get my attention. "Millie, you're a fast walker!" he exclaimed.

"Millie? My name is Amelia," I countered.

"Yeah, well." He winked at me. "I'm going to call you Millie. Does anyone else call you that?"

"No, but I ..." I started to argue with his statement, but he waved me off mid- sentence.

"Good, then it'll be our little thing," he said with a grin. "I was going to call you Em, but I realized your name started with an "A" and not an "E," so that didn't make much sense."

"So then you randomly came up with Millie?" I asked.

"No." He smiled. "I googled it."

I felt like telling him that there was no need for us to have any secret nicknames or aliases or whatever he wanted to call them; but I figured my resistance to it would only lead to more conversation, and I wanted our interaction to end before it even began.

"Anyways, here's your part of the assignment," he said as he handed me a stack of papers he had printed off in the library during our lab time. "Catch ya later." Then he gave me a playful punch on the arm before bouncing off to catch up with Anthony.

I closed my locker door and rested my head on it, squeezing my eyes shut. WHY did the obnoxious people always have to pick on me? Clearly it could only be for entertainment, especially since he was supposedly one of the "most popular boys" in the school, and – good God – if he knew my secrets, he'd probably rip me to shreds and spread it to the whole student body. I took a deep breath and headed off to my next class. If I kept ignoring him and showing no interest in even a friendship, he'd leave me to myself and move on to the next victim … right? Boys, especially the popular ones, don't waste their time with people who don't give them any attention.

The next day during sociology, we were sent mid-class to the computer lab to work on our assignment. I took my time getting up and gathering my things so I wouldn't be stuck surrounded by people I didn't want around me. With my luck, I would sit down in the computer lab in the corner and then five people would sit around me chatting each other up and breaking my concentration. If I walked in last, I would at least have the chance to be the lone duck in the back by myself. It was a brilliant plan, or would have been if it had worked out the way I wanted it to. Once again, I wasn't that lucky.

When I arrived at the lab, Anthony excitedly waved me over. I had to look behind me to see who the hell he had been waving at, because I was sure it wasn't me. I glanced over my shoulder, and I was only a little bit surprised to see there was no one behind me.

"Hey Millie, we saved you a seat!" Kellen exclaimed as he patted the seat between him and Anthony. A wide smile began to break across his face. I tried to smile a thanks in return, but all I managed was a crooked look of horror and confusion. Despite my reluctance I sat down and patiently waited for my computer to boot up. I quickly scrambled for my notebook and began examining a piece of paper that had absolutely nothing of interest on it, but doing so certainly made it look like I was too busy to hold a conversation with anyone.

In the middle of my fake concentration, a photo suddenly appeared on the sheet of paper. I glanced to my left, and Kellen was staring at his computer screen as though nothing had happened. I picked up the sepia-toned photo of a boy holding a soccer ball close to his face, his expression serious and meaningful.

"What's this?" I asked.

"My senior photo, obviously," Kellen responded without looking at me.

"Thank you?" I muttered in a querying tone, as I threw the photo in a book for safe keeping, trying to look as though I weren't moved by the thought, the gesture.

"There's something on the back – that's the important part. I didn't have any paper," he said with a wink, and with that, the class bell rang, and everyone darted out of the room.

He nudged my arm as he walked by. "Don't be afraid to use it – I gave it to you for a reason," he said before he, too, left the room. I waited until he was gone and then quickly took the photo out of the book and glanced at the back where his phone number was scribbled in black marker. My brow furrowed, and my heart skipped a beat; I quickly slipped it in the back of the book.

"No friends, Amelia. No means none," I mumbled under my breath as I exited the room.

chapter two

The next day at lunch I cautiously watched Kellen's table and wondered how the next hour's sociology class would go. I was trying my very best to seem as uninterested as possible, but he was more than persistent and a touch oblivious. Normally I would have perceived his actions as indicative of arrogance, but it didn't seem that way at all. It was as though he knew something I didn't, and when it came to me, he had no choice in the matter.

"Millie!" he said bluntly as I walked into the sociology classroom later that day.

"I really don't like that name ..." I confessed as I set my books down, hoping to divert anything else he might have planned to say.

"If I stopped calling you that, would you actually use the number I gave you and call me?" he asked. I blinked at his proposition.

"I guess … why, though?" unable to hide the confusion on my face.

He shook his head at me, and I suddenly felt like I did when my mother disapproved of something I was doing. Instead of explaining himself, he turned towards Anthony. "Are you coming to my game on Friday?" he asked him.

Anthony nodded and didn't look up from the papers on his desk.

"Alright, you are, too, then," he said as he turned back to me.

"Wha …" I started to argue back; the last place that I wanted to be was smushed in a massive crowd of people whom I didn't want to know me. I didn't need to be part of high school activities, to become someone who is seen or known. I needed to stay low-key.

Kellen waved me off and continued, "Anthony will pick you up at your car after school." He turned to Anthony who still hadn't looked up. "She parks in the lower lot; pick her up at the school doors and drive her down to her car to drop off her stuff?" he asked him.

Anthony again only nodded, as if it weren't something out of the ordinary.

Kellen turned back to me. "He'll keep you company before the game so you don't decide to bail last minute, and he will also sit with you so you don't have to find someone to buddy up with.

I'll find you afterwards. Sound good? Okay, good," he answered his own question before I had a chance to get a word in edgewise.

The teacher then closed the classroom door and announced we'd be starting our presentations and called Kellen, Anthony, and me up to the front of the classroom. Kellen tossed me his soccer ball as he walked by and winked.

"Now, who doesn't love a nice set of balls?" Kellen asked the class. I held my soccer ball up further in order to cover my face as Anthony snickers. It would figure I'd be the one lucky enough to get stuck with these two yahoos on a report about balls as the rest of the class giggled at the implications of our report. Everyone has an inner eighth grader, it seems. Finally Anthony composed himself long enough to explain to the class that we were doing our speech on the sociology of sports.

The next day I took my normal place at lunch, at a table full of juniors who had become my "lunch friends." I set down my tray, pulled out the blue plastic chair and was about to sit when someone picked my tray right back off of the table. I could tell immediately, because of the overpowering smell of A&F cologne, that it was Anthony, and I paused mid-sit to look back at him and ask why the hell he was stealing my food.

"Can't I just give you my lunch money? I don't feel like having to go through the line again," I asked in a serious tone.

"You're sitting with us today," he said nonchalantly and started to walk over to his table with my tray in his hand.

Panic overtook my body, and I scrambled to grab his shirt to stop him. "Anthony, I don't know any of those people!" I exclaimed in protest, but he ignored me and kept walking. He set my tray on the table and started pointing to people. "Matt, Scott, Michelle," he said and then took his seat next to me. Kellen walked up to the table and set his tray at an empty spot between Michelle and Anthony.

"That's Kellen," Anthony said, without looking up from his food.

I glanced around the room and spotted a few beady-eyed stares of disbelief coming from the girls sitting at the table. A tap on my foot brought my attention back to my situation, and as my brain connected the foot with the person to whom it belonged, I realized I was staring straight into Kellen's wide grin.

"Welcome to our table, Millie," he said without glancing away. He had his eyes locked straight onto mine and a wide grin takes over his face. My stomach flipped as I realized that I'm wasn't sure how much longer I'd be able to convince myself I wanted nothing to do with him.

***

I was going to Kellen's soccer game, I had no choice. Anthony did as he was told and picked me up from school that day, so I had no excuses for not going to the game and couldn't say I had simply forgotten. I jumped in to his SUV, and he smiled wide.

"We have about four hours," he said. "What do you want to do?"

I blinked. Four hours? What in the world had I agreed to? Or not agreed to, seeing as I never had a choice. "I really don't care," I said as he pulled out of the parking lot.

And that is a complete and utter lie, I thought to myself.

"Okay, good," he said. I could almost see the excitement pouring off of him. "I have some ideas, but first we need to stop by my house so I can get some stuff for tonight." I cringed at the thought of having to meet anyone from his family. How perfectly awkward. 'Oh, hello, who are you?' they'd say. 'Just nobody,' I'd reply.

I stood in his kitchen as he ran around gathering things. His brother came in to say a quick 'hello,' followed by his mom and sister. I just smiled politely and wished to God that I knew Anthony well enough to be angry at him for abandoning me with people I didn't know. When we got back into the truck, he smiled at me, trying very hard to contain his excitement. "Are you ready for it?" he asked. I look at him blankly. I hadn't the slightest clue what I needed to be ready for.

"I want to get my ear pierced ..." he said as he examined the upper part of his right earlobe in his rear-view mirror. "What do you think? Is that lame?" he asked.

The look on my face had to have been one of a deer in headlights, but I quickly shook my head 'no.'

"Alright," he said and smiled widely. "That's what we're going to do first!" He slapped my left leg and shifted his car into reverse, backing the SUV out of his driveway. As he exited his subdivision, he didn't even pause at a stop sign. I unwillingly croaked out a sound in response, and he started to laugh. "I've lived here five years, and never have I seen one car come from the other direction. Don't worry; you're safe with me. Kellen wouldn't have dubbed me your babysitter if I wasn't."

"Babysitter?!" I couldn't help but be annoyed by his use of words.

"Okay, wrong word. Hang on." He cranked up the radio and started to sing along. To my surprise, he had a really good singing voice. I pushed the volume button in to power the radio off.

"Babysitter?" I asked again, doubling the annoyance in my voice in order to drive home the message of *explain now*.

"Amelia, Kellen not only wanted to make sure you'd come tonight, but he wanted to make sure you were never alone or uncomfortable being there. I'm here to ensure that – most importantly – you show up and also to keep you company during the time he can't." When he finished talking, he looked over at me with a melancholy plea. Shock seemed to deprive me of words, so we sat in silence for a brief moment.

"Amelia?" Anthony's expression resembled that of a small child who had been sent to the corner for time-out.

24

"Hmm?"

"Can I have my music back?"

I giggled with a sigh of relief and pushed the power button on his radio. His face lit up, and he bounced in his seat a bit and quickly jumped into the middle of the song. I sat back and watched him as he sang. I wasn't sure if I should be impressed or making fun of him, so I just relaxed and enjoyed the show with a smile plastered on my face.

So we went, got our ears pierced, and by the time we left store (with matching piercings mind you), I suddenly didn't feel so tense any more. Anthony had a way of making me feel like we'd been best friends our entire lives and that this was entirely natural. We ate dinner at a local custard shop he used to work at and sat outside staring at the cars passing by, eating ice cream, and talking about anything and everything. Any time he'd start to ask me a question about my life or my life prior to my move to his school, I quickly countered with a question directed at him. I feared he'd eventually catch on, but he joined in my game and never pressed me on any of it.

***

In the bleachers that night there was no room left, not for one single body. Girls swooned over Kellen, and I carefully watched him running up and down the field, wondering how he didn't trip up over the ball or the sea of legs running beside him. At the sight of Kellen, my leg started to bounce in a flurry of nerves as my stomach started to once again flip in its limited space. I could see his gorgeous grin from where I was sitting, and I found myself trying very diligently to remember the sound of his voice and the break in his laugh.

Anthony elbowed me softly to get my attention, ripping me from my Kellen-induced trance.

"He has scouts coming to watch him next week. Might get a scholarship," he said. I raised my brows. All of this soccer talk, and Kellen never actually told me that he not only loved the game, but *was* the game.

Near the end of the game, I got antsy. I had been sitting for far too long, and the kids around me were getting wild. The game was close (but wasn't every soccer game "close"?) with only a few minutes left. I leaned towards Anthony. "I have to go to the bathroom real quick," I shouted, and he nodded in response, eyes focused on the intense game on the field. I started to make my way down the bleachers, trying not to trip over restless bodies flopping around like fish out of water. I rounded the corner, only to find Corbin with a crowd of kids who I was told were the "drug lords" of the school. A shudder rippled through my body, and I grimaced and felt all my muscles fall in disbelief with an exhausted exhale.

A shudder only meant one thing: I had ten days to figure out who needed help and what that person needed help with. The faulty hope that relocation to a new town and a new school would relieve me from my duties proved to be nothing but an illusion. And now it was shattered.

No matter where I went, it didn't change the fact that I was a Guardian chosen by the Powers That Be, and it was now my job to not only figure out who it was that needed my help, but what I was to save them from. I whipped around to be sure Corbin and his minions were the only people within my sight. No one else was in view. I stepped back slowly, into the shadows of the bleachers, and carefully counted. Including Corbin, there were five of them. I could do that; I had been faced with much greater challenges in past years. And on the bright side, at least the shudder hadn't come as I was sitting in the bleachers with hundreds of people.

I took a deep breath, scanned my surroundings quickly, and made a loud entrance into the tight circle they'd formed with their bodies.

"Corbin!?" I exclaimed with a huge smile on my face. "Corbin, oh my God, hi!" I said in my best I-have-no-clue-what's-going-on-and-am-a-total-ditz voice. Five sets of dark eyes peered back at me, clearly unamused and partially annoyed. Inside my chest, my heart was beating a thousand miles a minute. Not only did I have to figure out who was in need of help, but I also had to figure out who was the one sent here to work against me.

chapter three

After attempting to chat up Corbin and his friends, I gave up and headed off to the bathrooms. My mind is a whirlwind of chaos. What the hell was I going to do now? I only got a few months of peace and silence, and now it was all going to start up again. I leaned over the white porcelain sink and splashed cold water on my face. Guardianship was nothing short of completely exhausting.

The rules of the game were these: first, a shudder was the signal that someone was in need of my help. It wasn't always life or death, but sometimes a redirection of life choices in order to prevent chaos in the future. At the time of the shudder, I would know two things for sure: I was both in the presence of the person in need of help and the person sent here by the Devil himself to stop me from helping. The Devil's Advocates were not obvious to the naked eye; His people resembled any ordinary human being.

But they weren't ordinary human beings, and they had just as much power as I to steer the person in need in the opposite direction of the path to which I was supposed to lead them.

Of course, the Powers That Be wouldn't leave me here to undertake such a great responsibility without help. During the week I had to help the person in need, I had periodic heightened senses and a memory that was relentless. Best of all, during my sleeping hours, I had the ability to revisit the places I had been and rummage through the scenes for more clues as to what I needed to do. There was no time that was wasted.

Just because I had been through this a thousand times before didn't make it any easier. The crowd outside erupted with a cheer, and I buckled to the ground, covering my ears and wincing in pain. It would take a bit to become accustomed to hearing the world at an amplified level. It felt like someone had broadcast the cheering as loudly as they could in the small space I occupied. I rushed out of the bathroom and ran straight into one of the soccer players. Completely taken by surprise, I bounced off of him and fell backwards onto the grass.

"Are you alright?!" he asked, eyes wide and reached his hand down to me to help me up.

"Yeah, I'm fine," I said, surprised at the clarity and strength in my voice considering my current situation. "Apparently 'look before you leap' isn't just a saying, huh?" I offered a smile. He let out a small sigh of laughter and walked past me back towards the game.

My body trembled as I walked back to the bleachers, only to find people swarming out of the game as though there were a fire. I was stuck in a mob of people as the players walked by. There was a group of teenage girls next to me giggling and shrieking over Kellen. I cut through the crowd and started to walk to my car quickly. I caught Kellen out of the corner of my eye; he was walking slowly across the field with his coach. I picked up my pace, begging God to not let him see me.

"Millie!" he yelled out. I froze and slowly turned around.

"Good game," I shot back, walking backwards slowly.

A huge grin spread across his face. "Thanks for actually coming!" he said. I nodded and turned to walk faster to my car, praying sleep would shed some clarity on who it was that needed my help.

"Hey, hang on a second!" he called after me and I stopped, knowing if I didn't have a quick conversation with him, I'd never hear the end of it. I heard him inch closer; with my heightened hearing, I could tell when he was exactly within my reach. I turned to face him just in time to see a shudder ripple through his body.

He looked up at me, expecting me to think nothing of it and was instead met with a look of horror and confusion. With my eyes practically popping out of their sockets and my mouth unwillingly agape, I quickly scanned the crowd around us. Corbin and his punk friends were here, along with people still filtering out of the bleachers and a few soccer players standing around chatting with friends and family. I glanced back at Kellen, who was taking the same inventory of the people around us. His eyes met mine, and for the first time since I'd met him, he wasn't wearing a goofy grin, and his eyes weren't lit with promise.

"Kellen ..." I began to say, and he grabbed my wrist and started to pull me towards the parking lot.

"Not here," he barked back and quickly scribbled an address on the back of my hand before breaking out into a slight jog to his car.

When I got to my car, I was a mess. My body felt as though confusion and fear would tear me from the inside out. I started to drive, yet I didn't know where I was going. I took a few back roads and wound through a wooded area. I thought Kellen lived close by, but I wasn't sure. Was he leading me to his house? I squinted at the road name on the back of my hand. I grabbed his photo from above my visor and turned to the number on the back. I was in the middle of nowhere at a T in the road, but there weren't any cars around me, so I just waited for some sign from God telling me which way to go. My car made three dinging noises, and I glanced down to see I was almost out of gas. I slowly pulled away from the stop sign and headed towards the nearest gas station, which just happened to be on the very road I was looking for.

Leaning against my car, my brain was running in circles, and although I was staring hard at the changing numbers of the pump, I wasn't actually paying any attention to them. The image of Kellen shuddering rumbled through my head. This was mere coincidence. It had to be. There was no way ... I never had met anyone like myself. Did others exist? I shivered and wondered if I was imagining things when I heard my name being called. I turned towards the source of the sound to see Kellen was standing at the trunk of my car. The sullen look on his face told me the incident earlier really did mean something.

"I needed gas," I mumbled when the silence became unbearable. I wasn't used to seeing Kellen so serious, and I wasn't sure what to think of it. He nodded in response and took a minute before talking. I glanced back at the pump, thinking to myself that I had to have found the slowest pump in the world.

"I'm going to head back to my car; follow me to the end of the road when you're done." With that he turned and walked towards his yellow Cavalier. The gas pump came to a stop, startling me out of thought, and I grabbed for it suddenly, wishing it would've taken longer. What was I going to say to him?

It took me all of a minute to reach the end of the road. I got out of my car and leaned against it. My body was still humming but my mind was suddenly blank. Kellen got out of his car and leaned against mine next to me.

"What happened?" he asked after a moment of silence. I glanced over at him with a confused look on my face. Why did he get to ask questions? I wasn't about to spill my secret and have him look back to me with horror, wondering what the hell it was I was talking about. I remained silent and just stared back at him.

He was patient, but he eventually realized I wasn't going to answer. We sat in silence for what seemed to be an eternity when he stood up and started to step away. I was about to breathe a sigh of relief, but he pivoted to stand in front of me, placed his feet on either side of mine very carefully and, with only a foot of space between us, looked at me and asked again, "What happened?"

I was no longer calm or bored or able to breathe. My body started to hum, and my heart felt like it was going to tear through my chest at any moment. I squirmed at his invasion of personal space. I was trapped, but what was worse was that the only thing I could think was he was not close enough. The first words of the book I never wrote started something like this: "Everyone needs human interaction. Everyone thrives off of it, everyone learns from it, and everyone can become a better person because of it." The words were the truth, but I wasn't exactly your average human. I had a responsibility to the world, to protect people and keep them safe. There wasn't time for something as mundane as a relationship. Any former relationship I'd had wasn't actually a relationship at all. It appeared to be so to the outside world, but in all actuality, what looked like a relationship was my attempt to save people sent to me. So I'd save them and move on with my life.

As a Guardian I wasn't allowed to "have." That didn't mean I didn't yearn to be like everyone else. Most of my days were completely exhausting and nothing short of mentally draining. At the end of the day, I wanted to drive straight home and curl up next to someone who would follow me as I walked through the door and picked up the pieces of myself I'd been trying to shed my entire life. I wanted someone to gather me into his arms and say, "Don't worry, I'll take care of you. Just be."

Instead I'm constantly bombarded with phone calls from people who are very desperate, people fleeing from their lives and running straight to me, begging me to rescue those bits and pieces of themselves they have lost.

Keeper of souls. Puzzle solver. Heart mender. Truth was, I was falling apart at the seams, desperate for that one person to help me hold myself together. These thoughts often ran rapidly through my head as though they were on a mission to destroy me. They made me weaker than I had already made myself. It was like poison. It didn't stay secluded in one small part of my body; instead it spread until it had no place left to go.

I suddenly didn't feel like there was any reason to keep anything secret from him. I looked up at him and frowned at the seriousness written in his expression. At that moment the only thing I could think was I would do anything to break the straight line his mouth had formed and make it transform into his infectious smile. He started to shift his weight from one foot to the other, tapping the outer edge of his Adidas sneakers against my Vans. He wasn't going anywhere until I spoke, so I told him: I told him about my duties as a Guardian and about the shudder I had experienced a few minutes before he had. He listened but didn't say a word, and the expression on his face stayed stern the whole time. I watched him carefully but I couldn't tell if he was hearing this all for the first time or if I was telling him a mirror of his own life.

After throwing my words around in his head for a minute or two he spoke. "And your dreams?" he asked. My body fell in relief. He wouldn't know to ask about them if he didn't already know the answer.

"I'm the puppetmaster. I can go anywhere I once was. I can observe the scene and pick out pieces I didn't notice the first time."

He nodded. "Well, I guess we get to it then," he said as he backed a few steps away from me and ran his hands through the spikes of his hair causing it to fall into a light fluff. He shook his head and rubbed his face, clearly trying to concentrate. He opened his eyes and blinked hard a few times. "Who was there the first time, when you experienced it?"

I closed my eyes to see the scene and answer. "Corbin Blake and four other guys, but I don't know their names."

"Corbin was in view during mine too ..." He started to pace in front of me. "Just four others?" I nodded. "Well, I guess we can't do anything until tomorrow. You can point out the other four to me and I can name them. Go back tonight and make sure there was no one you missed. I'll go back and try to pull more names from the crowd at my scene, but there were more people there so it'll be a bit harder."

He quickly cut the space between us and had one hand propping himself up on the car behind me. He stares deep in to my eyes and for a minute neither of us speak. He picked up a lock of my hair and started to twirl it, following the bends of the curl. "You came to McHenry High to escape the Guardianship, didn't you?" The empathy in his voice was genuine. I don't answer but he nodded at the expression I couldn't hide. "I'm sorry it didn't work." He picked up another curl and placed it further away from my face. "But I'm not sorry that you're here." My stomach dropped and I struggled to swallow. His gaze was so intense that I felt as though I might melt into a puddle of nothing at his feet.

I cleared my throat. "I should, ah, I should go home. Get to bed, see if I can figure anything out." He pushed himself away from the car and gave me my space. I scrambled for the door handle before he had any time to give me any awkward goodbye. He immediately headed for his car.

"Amelia?"

I look back to see him standing between our vehicles. My stomach dropped at the sound of my name. I hadn't heard him use it in its entirety since the day we met. My face twisted in an unexpected grimace. "Did you ever fail?"

I nodded slowly. Sometimes it was near impossible to save a life, especially with the Advocates working just as hard to make sure you failed. He nodded back at me and slipped into his car. I watched him speed off and sat in the silence for a few moments staring at my steering wheel. What the hell just happened?!

chapter four

I couldn't sleep. Problem being, I knew I needed to in order to revisit the scene. But no matter how hard I tried to concentrate on falling asleep, I could only replay my conversations with Kellen over and over again. I watched his face fall and stay sullen the entire night. No matter how much I didn't want to admit it, I missed his smile.

I finally drifted off around one a.m. and was thrown into some wild crazy dream about drinking tea on a beach in California. I must have been tired because it took a bit before I actually absorbed my surroundings and realized I wasn't where I needed to be. "Wait," I said as I jumped up from my seat on a wooden crate. Everyone around me stopped to look at me in confusion. All was quiet and a cat meowed. I looked over to where the cat was sitting and shook my head. "I have somewhere else to be," I told all who were listening. They nodded and I closed my eyes.

When I opened them again, I was standing huddled under the bleachers a few feet from Corbin and his friends. I took an extra minute to memorize their faces so I'm able to point them out to Kellen in the morning. Corbin glanced back at me with obvious concern, a plea of sorts. I froze before realizing he couldn't really see me and there was no reason to stay motionless. Something flew through the air within their circle and I saw someone hold out their foot to catch it.

Hack. They were playing hacky-sack. I panned the rest of the area, looking for any other sign of life. There was a possibility someone was there I may have not noticed the first time, but no one is. I inched closer to Corbin's group but they weren't saying much, just staring through glazed eyes at the hacky sack flying through the air. A guy with dreads threw his body at the hacky sack to save it from exiting the circle. As he moved I could hear a faint rattle in his pocket. "I know that sound," I said out loud and focused hard on matching the sound with memory. My mind quickly sifted through a few dozen small moments of my every day until it fell on my after breakfast routine. I put my dishes away and reached for my pills. In memory I see myself grab the bottle from the cupboard, causing the pills to shift up against the cap and then back to the bottom of the bottle.

The guy had a bottle of pills in his pocket.

A horn sounded an alarm over the PA, and everyone looked up at the speakers. Corbin turned to me. "Time to wake up

Amelia," and with that, he and his friends all started toward the school.

***

That morning, I rushed to get out of the door and to school a few minutes early. I felt like I had selfishly wasted time by having a pow-wow with Kellen the night before instead of going home to analyze my current case. If for some reason this particular project failed, it was going to be my fault. I headed straight to my locker and began to rummage through it, as though I had a purpose in doing so. A voice from behind my opened locker door jolted me from thought and caused me to jump back in reflex.

"You know, technically, you should have heard me coming …" Kellen drawled with a raised brow.

I scowled at him. "I was too deep in thought to decipher specific sounds. It's loud in here; it just sounds like a blur of noise right now," I snapped back as I grabbed my books from my locker and slammed the door shut. I looked back at him, but he had a cocky look on his face, so I started to walk away. I knew he was right behind me because the smell of him was stronger because my senses were heightened.

"Well … did you find anything last night?" He struggled to keep up with my pace.

I stopped and stared at him in annoyance. "I never said I wanted to be your partner, Kellen. I can do this on my own. Or you can do it on your own. Or … whatever." I shook my head in frustration and started to walk away again, but he grabbed my hand.

"Millie," he said softly.

Despite the fact that all of the members of the student body were exercising their voices in the hallways of McHenry, his voice was the only one I heard. I abruptly stopped, and my heart jumped into my throat. I turned to face him, but my eyes were fixed on our intertwined hands. I paused for a moment, unsure of what to say, my heart beating loudly in my chest. I needed to walk away from him, but I couldn't convince my body to obey. The first bell rang, startling me back to reality, the flood of noise slowly seeping back into my consciousness. Kellen started to lead me toward my first class, our hands still joined.

"Did you get a good look at them last night?"

I nodded and looked around; there were too many people to be able to single out four of them.

"Okay, we'll try to find them at lunch time, when everyone is at least stationary," he stated as he looked up at the numbers above a classroom. I, too, looked up and realized we'd stopped in front of my first hour English class. Before I realized what he was doing, he leaned in, our cheeks now close enough he might have been able to feel that my entire body was humming.

"Go to the Homecoming dance with me," he whispered into my ear. He brought his face close to mine, mere inches away, and watched me carefully for an answer. Despite the swarm of people around us, it suddenly felt like we were the only people who existed. I was afraid to speak, fearing that doing so would bring reality crashing back down upon us, so I simply nodded, and he walked away.

My second-hour study hall was with Corbin. I sat at our usual table after going through the ala carte line to grab some breakfast. I picked at my bagel as I watched kids slowly trickle into the cafeteria. When the second bell rang and Corbin still hadn't slipped into his normal seat, I frowned.

"It's quiet time people!" the study hall monitor announced from the front of the room. I opened my book to start my math homework, but was distracted by the sound of a bouncing leg from somewhere in the room. I turned and panned the tables looking for the culprit and was surprised to see it was coming from the boy with the dreads who had been with Corbin the night before. I looked back at the study hall monitor who was getting up from her table to fill her water bottle. I quietly gathered my things and nonchalantly walked over to dread-dude's table.

"Mind if I sit with you?" I whispered. The guy with dreads looked up at me with twisted confusion. "Corbin usually sits with me but he isn't here today … if I sit alone I'll fall asleep," I lied. He raised his brows as if my confession impressed him and motioned for me to have a seat. "By the way, I'm Amelia," I mentioned as I held out a hand. He looked down at it and muttered quietly, "I know who you are."

fly

"Quiet, people!" The study hall monitor was back from filling her water with horrible timing. I had been attempting to get a name out of him to no avail. I sulked in my seat and pretended to be concentrating on my math book. I stole glances at him when I knew he was deep in concentration. He was slender, and his cheek bones were high and prominent, his dark dreads always pulled back and tied into a ponytail.

He flipped a page in his history book, and I glanced up at the sound of metal being dragged across the table. His hand stopped to rest on the right side of the book, cradling it, just enough for me to see the familiar symbol of a red snake wrapped around a staff. I squinted to see the inscription. The bracelet read *Taran Michaels, 10/1/1994, Hypertension.* Alright, now I knew why he had a bottle of pills in his pocket, but that didn't rule out the possibility he was the one who needed help. I scribbled the information down in my notebook and wrote "High blood pressure + medication + street drugs = death?" I tapped my pen on my notebook, and my mind drifted to my conversation that morning with Kellen.

"Oh God," I thought to myself and winced. I had told him I'd go to the Homecoming dance with him! I'd never been to a dance before. I was also fairly certain the last dress I purchased was for my eighth grade graduation. My mind started to flood with panic. I didn't have a dress, I didn't have friends to go dress shopping with, and I had absolutely no clue as to when this dance even was. I turned the page and quickly scribbled *When's the homecoming dance?* and then turned the notebook to Taran. He looked at it, a scowl still on his face, and quickly wrote back. When he pushed the notebook back to me, it read *How the hell should I know?* in neat handwriting. I smiled nervously at him and nodded. Touche, Taran.

It suddenly dawned on me he might know where Corbin was, and Corbin was the one person I really needed to talk to. The easiest way to figure out who the other four boys were would be to just simply ask who he was with last night and save us some time trying to find them and put names to faces.

Where's Corbin today? I wrote and once more pushed the notebook to him. He rolled his eyes and drew a huge circle around his previous answer. My face reddened, and I pulled the notebook back and flipped it back to my Taran list and wrote *Jerk*. I flipped back to my math homework, giving up on project Taran. I guess I'd just have to wait until lunch to try to find out more.

I had barely sat down in my third-hour history class when a loud wail came in through the PA. The teacher attempted to speak over the sound, but because I refused to remove my hands from my ears, I only managed to hear we were having a fire drill and learned no details. I followed the class out of the door and across the parking lot and watched as people started to huddle in small groups. I had wandered into the group of people I used to eat lunch with before Anthony had prompted my new seating arrangement.

Nothing had changed; they all talked rapidly, and I attempted to blend in with them by laughing along with them at the right times. I didn't talk, but I didn't want to fall prey to anyone wandering around looking for a friend.

I shuffled from foot to foot, staring at the brick building, willing it to announce for us to come back inside. The girls behind me giggled during a conversation about Kellen and Anthony, whom I noticed were a few groups away from us. I tried to rub the tension from my face and glanced back up at the school once more before turning around to face the chatty girls.

"Who are you guys talking about?" I asked with fake curiosity in my eyes.

"Only the hottest boys in the school!" they squealed in rapid response. They pointed over at Kellen and Anthony, and my hand went straight to my ear, absentmindedly fiddling with my new piercing. One girl dared the other to go over and talk to them. I glanced over again; Kellen had wandered away, but Anthony remained standing in a small, huddled group of boys.

"Yeah right!" the other girl exclaimed.

I glanced back at the brick building and rolled my eyes. How long did a fire drill take? Honestly.

"I'll do it," I chirped. They both glanced at me with wide eyes.

"Well … we were wagering a dollar," one girl told me. I raised my brows at this. That, right there, was Rice Krispie money which I had conveniently forgotten this morning. Lunch was not lunch without a Rice Krispie treat. I grinned and rolled my eyes at the two of them. "He's just a person," I reminded them in a motherly fashion as I walked away. I glanced back to see both of them standing closely together, staring at me like they were watching me walk to my death.

I gently tapped Anthony on the shoulder as if I had never talked to him before and was approaching him for the first time. "Before you say anything," I quickly started, "I am over here on a dare from a few girls behind me ... they were wild about what would happen if they came and – gasp – talked to you, so play along?" I asked, and he nodded. I could see what they saw in him; he did look like someone who could be cast as the heartthrob in a teen TV show. His hair was as black as night and always seemed to fall perfectly, and his smile flashed a perfect set of bright white teeth. The failure to shave on a daily basis gave him the rough-around-the-edges look that most girls swooned over. It was the teenage version of a five o'clock shadow.

"Going to the homecoming dance, Amelia?" he asked with a playful nudge. My face reddened and he laughed. "I'll take that as a yes." A smile broke across his face. I could practically hear the heartbeats of the girls watching us. "Any chance I can get you in on the decorating committee?" I looked up at him and his expression was sly.

fly

"I'm not quite sure I'll have time," I replied, and it wasn't a lie. I needed to focus on my case. I wasn't about to throw my Guardianship out of the window for some stupid dance I hadn't even known about until this morning.

"Well, we have a busy week next week," he started. I scrunched my face in confusion, and he clarified by counting off activities on his fingers. "Kellen's big game is next week; we have to decorate for the dance and the homecoming football game. By the way, I'll pick you up at your car after school Thursday so we can go and pick up supplies before we decorate. Make sure you don't make any plans at all that day because I have a funny feeling it'll take all night." He winked at me.

I rolled my eyes and shook my head slightly. I didn't think he was going to take my answer of 'I'm busy,' and apparently I was right. We stood at a comfortable distance, and I crossed my arms.

"How long do these things usually last?" I asked him, noticing a chill in the air.

"Long enough to be worth it." He smiled, and with that the PA announcer started to tell us all to come back inside. I glanced back over at the giddy girls, and they were staring at me, jaws slack. I clenched my neck and jaw in an "Oh my God!" valley-girl way. I giggled under my breath; thank God someone was good for entertainment around here.

48

Anthony hit me on the arm as people started to slowly flood toward the door. "By the way, heard you and Kellen were dating now," he said as he started to follow the crowd. I froze in my tracks. How the hell could a rumor like that even get around? He was going to think I said something to someone; he was going to hate me. On the other hand, if he was going to hate me, I wouldn't have to worry about actually falling for him. I surprised myself by not knowing which of the two scenarios I feared most.

"Who told you that?" I frantically asked.

Anthony turned back around to see me trailing behind him. "Kellen did."

I stopped dead in my tracks. Noticing the way I was humming with excitement at his response, a smile started to slowly spread across my face.

chapter five

I approached lunch with caution. I slowly went through the line wondering to myself where I was supposed to sit. Had yesterday's change of tables been permanent, or did I need to be invited over to Kellen and Anthony's table again? I was deep in thought while I exited the line only to have my tray taken out of my hands.

"Really?!" I looked up from my empty hands to see the back of Kellen's head and promptly followed him to an empty table in the corner of the room. He set down my tray. "We need to be somewhere that we can see the whole room and the courtyard." He pointed to his right out of the bay windows, and I saw people huddled in groups around marble tables. "I had to cut you off; it would've been awkward had we sat down at our usual table and then got up to sit somewhere else."

I nodded. "Yeah, makes perfect sense. Except, oh wait, I don't have a 'usual table.' And dating? Really Kellen? Don't two people have to be in agreement in order to be dating?" I was still standing beside the chair I was supposed to be occupying, and Kellen had somehow already eaten half of his burger.

"We are in agreement. You just won't admit it. Sit down." I opened my mouth to disagree with his statement, but I decided against it and sat down. I didn't have time for arguments; we were sitting there for a reason. Guardianship came before all else.

"I talked to one of the boys today. Corbin wasn't here today for study hall, so I took the liberty of sitting by one of the boys I recognized from last night." Kellen was leaning back in his chair; his burger had completely disappeared, and he was slowly eating his fries. He said nothing, so I continued. "His name is Taran, and I didn't get much out of him; he wasn't particularly chatty."

Kellen sat up and put his arms on the table, leaning closer to me and staring intensely at my face. I quickly wiped my mouth with my hand. "What?"

"You have the most beautiful eyes," he stated in a very serious tone.

"Kellen!" My jaw tensed. "Can you please pay attention?"

"I am paying attention." He leaned back again and popped a fry into his mouth. "Study hall, Taran, uncooperative."

"Well, did you see anything last night?" He shook his head 'no' and broke open his Cherry Coke.

I turned and started to scan the crowd for the other three boys. The cafeteria was wide, and without standing, it was difficult to see people. "There!" I exclaimed and pointed to a boy with bleached-blond hair. Kellen looked at me with raised brows. "Ugh, hang on." I turned back to count the number of tables, vertical and horizontal, before I reached the boy. "Four tables down and two to the left," I told him. He craned his neck to find the table I'd pointed out to him. "Okay …" He waited for me to continue, but never took his eyes off of the table. "Bleached- blond hair and blue hoodie and the bald one to the right of him," I finished.

"The blond is Sam Miller, and the bald one is Adam Moore." He leaned back again and took a swig of his soda.

"Do you have any classes with them?"

"Yeah, seventh hour Bio with Sam, but none with Adam."

"Okay, well, can you talk to him?"

"I can try, but we're in the middle of a project, and we don't have much time to wander the classroom striking up random conversations with people you've never been seen talking to before." I rolled my eyes at him, and he threw up his hands in defense. "I didn't say I wasn't going to try – I obviously will – I'm just saying it's not exactly going to be easy. Do I get something if I succeed?" He raised his eyebrows, as though he were impressed with his own proposition.

"Kellen, seriously." I set my burger down and pushed my tray to the middle of the table.

"I am serious. If I succeed, I think I deserve a kiss. What's wrong with your burger?" He frowned at my mostly full tray of food.

"It's pink." I grimaced.

"And?"

"And if you succeed, I'll kiss you." A smile broke across my face, and my heart started to beat noticeably harder. "On the cheek," I add.

Kellen shrugged, the smile only getting bigger. "I'll take what I can get." He grabbed my burger and bit into it after sliding a blue-wrapped package across the table. A Rice Krispie Treat slid to a halt in front of me.

"Anyone else? We're missing one person." I glanced out at the crowd again and shook my head.

"Alright, keep your eyes peeled in the halls then." He got up and grabbed my tray, and the warning bell rang immediately after, as though he had known it was time to go.

"See you sixth hour." He winked at me and quickly shuffled to catch up with Anthony.

When I entered sociology that day, Kellen and Anthony were patiently waiting for me.

"Hey, so Coach said I couldn't do it, but he loves me too much to punish me for it, so I'm going to anyways," Kellen was saying excitedly as I took my seat in class. He had gotten most of the words out before I had even been able to sit down.

"Do what?" I inquired, confused on all accounts. I felt like I had somehow missed half of the conversation.

"Dye my hair." A devilish grin started to spread over his face. "So I have one question then, red or blue?" he asked with wild eyes.

I smiled and I shook my head. He hadn't failed to shock me with his antics, not even once.

"Surprise me," I answered, thinking he was going to look ridiculous either way and was most likely going to also get in trouble either way. Just then the teacher claimed our attention as she began class, and I thanked God he didn't have the opportunity to press for a more concrete answer from me.

"Millie," I heard a whisper come from close behind me. I turned my head to tell him to shush, but he continued before I could silence him.

"There's a barn party tomorrow night; will you go with me?" I glanced back at the teacher, who still had her back to the class. The sound of chalk clinking against the board rapidly proved to be mildly distracting. I pulled out my notebook and wrote *I actually get a choice in the matter this time?* and slipped it onto his desk. Minutes later, he reached around me and slapped the notebook back onto my desk, causing the teacher to turn around and look at us. My face reddened. So much for not disturbing the class. She turned back around and continued to write. I look down at the paper. His handwriting was sloppy, and it took a minute before I could actually translate the scribble into words. *Nope. Meet me at my house at 8. The address is 627 Oak Drive. I'll be home alone, so just let yourself in. I'll be downstairs. Oh, and by the way, have I told you that you have beautiful eyes?*

I stayed completely still, fearing if I moved in the slightest, Kellen would be able to see the tremble running through me. This still didn't feel like a good idea, being friends with Kellen, dating Kellen, merely conversing with Kellen. I was capable of thinking these thoughts, but actually listening to them was a whole different story.

I walked out of my sociology class in what felt like a drunken haze. In fact, the whole day felt like it was yesterday. Or even better, that it hadn't happened at all. I had been doing so well at deflecting Kellen; what had happened? Yes, I had gone to his game. I could have said no, but at the time I thought I had somehow checked myself out of Guardianship and had no reason to fear being around people.

I cringed at my own thoughts. It wasn't that I didn't like to help people, save lives. I did. Succeeding in a life redirection was the most amazing feeling in the world. A few months ago I had run into a man whose life I had saved from a suicide attempt, and it was an overwhelming feeling of pride and joy to know I was the reason he was standing in front of me at that very moment. I was unable to do anything other than smile back at him so hard that my face actually felt stretched-out afterwards. I not only loved saving people, but I lived for it. The thing that got me was the fear of not succeeding, having to see the devastation that it could cause, knowing I actually was responsible for other people's pain because I wasn't able to succeed. I mean, I wasn't stupid—I understood it wasn't me who had driven them to do the things they did. I understood I didn't directly, purposely cause people pain. But I indirectly did, and it sucked the entire life force out of me.

My thoughts consumed me for the next few class periods. I robotically copied down notes and answered any questions when I was called on to do so, but I wasn't actually listening. Instead, I was running through all of my past scenarios, trying to pull out common denominators and apply them to the cases I failed and the case I was currently in. Every once in a while, Kellen would pop into my head, his infectious smile, his forceful charm. At first I would smile and start to chew on my bottom lip and daydream about what it would be like to just completely give in to his persistent attempts to bring us together. Then there would be a sudden rush of the emotional devastation my last friendships brought which intruded into my happy, optimistic mood. My mind became dark, cloudy even. Fear hovered overhead in a glowing, green haze. Emotions were rolling through me like the ocean when it's angry after a storm. Waves of fear and despair were crashing into me like they had every intention of ruining the very thing that held me together. I shut my eyes and hunched down in my seat, attempting to gather myself and my thoughts at the same time. My thoughts were running away from me, throwing obstacles along the way, hoping I would trip and fall. I knew I needed to get up and distract myself or else I'd just quit trying to catch up to them and let them win. If I closed my eyes, could I make people disappear?

"You could have saved him," a woman's voice bit through my thoughts. I lifted my head up off the desk, remembering how it felt to be thrown off guard by hearing those words. Rightfully so, since I had caused her to lose her only son.

The bell rang to signal the change to our last class, but I remained still in my seat, willing the world away.

I somehow managed to drag myself to my ninth-hour math class. It was the only classroom that was tucked away on the upper floor of the school. The rest of the rooms on that floor were for choir and band rehearsals and most often stayed vacant during the second half of the day. I sat down at my desk and looked up at the board. The teacher had scribbled *Quiz TODAY!* in very large letters, filling every vacant space of green on the board. I closed my eyes and exhaled; I didn't have the energy for everything that was happening.

"Yes!" Mr. Cooper boomed as he entered the room. "We're having a quiz today!" The class groaned its disapproval in unison. Mr. Cooper mocked our whining faces and smiled. "If you all don't stop whining, I can't tell you the good news …" He winked. The class fell silent, and Mr. Cooper grinned widely, showing us every single one of his pearly whites. "You're having a quiz and you may find a partner." He held a finger up to stop us from glancing sideways at our best friends. "A partner OF the opposite sex. You may use your notes, and notes only on this quiz. You have the class period to finish." He stood staring at us, and we all watched him carefully for permission to scurry off and find a partner. I rested my head on the desk. I didn't even talk to anyone in this class, much less know who it is I was supposed to trust enough to complete a test with. He must have signaled us with a hand gesture because I heard everyone getting up to rearrange their seats.

"Please let there be an odd amount of people," I mumble to myself. Just then, I heard someone slide into the desk in front of me.

"We meet again," I heard a male voice say. I looked up in the hope that whoever it was, was talking to someone else. No such luck, once again. He held his hand out. "I'm Paul," he stated as he coolly shook my hand.

"Amelia," I mumbled back.

"Look before you leap," he noted with a grin plastered on his face.

"Huh?"

"You ran into me at the soccer game." He raised his eyebrows. "Literally."

"Oh! At the bathrooms!" I could feel the blood rushing to my cheeks. I cursed my horrible habit of trying to accommodate for embarrassing moments by saying something clever. I haven't once succeeded at the clever part.

Mr. Cooper slid a test onto Paul's desk and nodded at us. "Good luck!"

"Did you take notes?" Paul asked.

I nodded, thinking back to my study hall earlier today. Was that today? God, it felt like yesterday or ten years ago.

"Good, I did too, and hopefully between the both of us we'll have enough info to get through this." He opened his notebook, and I started to do the same.

Flipping through the pages, my attention caught on the page I was taking notes about Taran on. There was more scribble than the small amount I had written. I furrowed my brows to try and decipher the words.

Kellen Anders:

Good looking

Killer wardrobe

Heart-stopping smile

Is this love?

;)

"Alright, question one." Paul's voice broke into my thoughts, and I quickly turned the page. I could feel my face heating up and wondered if I was starting to look like a lobster to everyone else. That would have to be the last time I left my

fly

notebook vulnerable to Kellen. *Note to self: rip the page out if you want to communicate with Kellen through writing.*

I finally found my math notes. "Okay, shoot," I told Paul and with that, we dove into the world of numbers.

The entire class finished the test within the first twenty minutes of class, so we were asked to socialize quietly for the remainder of the period while our teacher graded our work. I expected Paul to flee my company at the first opportunity to, but to my dismay he stayed put.

"You're new this year, right?" Paul leaned against the bar of his desk, stretched out his legs, and crossed his arms. I nodded in response and prayed to God he wasn't really hoping to talk to me for the rest of the class period. I nervously glanced up at the teacher in the hope that Paul would be discouraged by my lack of attention.

But he wasn't. "Did your family move to town then?" he continued, despite my effort.

"No." I shake my head. "Just me. I moved in with my grandma."

"Any siblings?"

I nodded. How many questions could one person ask before he got the hint that the conversation was becoming one sided?

"Siblings are a pain in the ass sometimes. Always stealing your stuff, ratting on you for your mistakes." He grew silent and watched me as if needing a response. I squirmed in my seat and

61

decided he wasn't going to give up. I figured I might as well make this less painful. After all, there was no harm in a conversation, right?

"At least you have someone to talk to when you get home. I only have my grandma, and half the time she hasn't the slightest clue about what I'm talking about. I mean, she listens, but she doesn't really get it. Too much time has passed; she doesn't remember what it's really like being a teenager." I bit my lip and rolled my eyes when I was done speaking. *God Amelia, could you maybe just make something up next time, like a short answer that doesn't involve emotions?* I really sucked at this whole "not connecting with people" rule I had made myself. The rule had a purpose, and that purpose would be served. But only if I followed it.

Paul thankfully changed the conversation to something less personal, and we spent the last ten minutes in class discussing our thoughts and theories on a Sci-Fi show we both indulged in on Thursday nights. By the end of class, I was leaning toward him and becoming animated in my input to the conversation. The bell rang, and I smiled as I threw my books into my bag.

"Hey, you should message me next week after you watch the new episode. I don't know anyone else who watches the show, much less has seen every single one." He slipped a small folded piece of paper into the hand that was gripping my backpack. He started to walk out of the classroom, but stopped at the doorway, blocking my exit. I turned to see that I was last to leave the room.

"One more question." He tipped his head, and his soft brown hair slid across his forehead.

I looked up at him and noticed his eyes were so dark that they could pass for black. It seemed to give his gaze more intensity, and I grew suddenly nervous.

"Are you going to the dance next week?"

I winced at his question, hoping he was just taking a poll. I pressed my lips together and nodded.

He smiled in hope. "Have a date?"

"Kellen asked me this morning." The words fell from my mouth before I realized that a 'yes' would have sufficed.

Paul looked up at the door frame and shifted against the left side, allowing room for me to pass. "I didn't think I'd be that lucky," he said as I passed through.

"See you next week, Paul," I said nonchalantly, trying to ease the awkwardness. As soon as I was out of his view, I picked up my pace and headed straight for the parking lot. The weekend had finally arrived, and I couldn't have been happier.

chapter six

I wasn't looking forward to sleep that night. To say I was exhausted would be an extreme understatement. All I wanted to do was get rest, but there was work to be done that *had* to be done. Sleep was rest for most, but to a Guardian it was work. I wanted to close my eyes, see nothing but black space, and fall into a sleep so deep I'd wake up in the same exact spot I had fallen asleep in.

When I opened my eyes after falling asleep, I was back under the bleachers once more. Even my dream self knew how tired I was, because instead of being crouched down under the metal bars as I was the last time, this time I was sitting in the stone. I rolled on my left leg to inch out of the stone and onto the grass, and when I went to lift myself off of the ground, I was facing the bathrooms at the top of the hill. Corbin and his friends were straight to my right. I squinted up at the bathrooms.

"Hello?" I yelled out, and the person entering the men's room quickly glanced backwards, but then slipped into the bathroom before I could tell who it was. Someone else was here. Someone unaccounted for. I glanced back at Corbin's group and counted five boys. There was a sixth person.

My stomach took a hard drop as my mind flashed back to that night.

Paul. Paul was in the bathrooms; I had run into him on my way out. I quietly walked up to the small concrete building and stood close to the men's room door. I felt uneasy about entering it, even in my dreams, so I stayed outside and strained to hear any type of conversation. The metal of the door was cold on my cheek, and the sound of his voice through the door was muffled. I felt like I was part of a scene in *Peanuts*, listening to the teacher talking to her students.

He was on his cell phone; I was sure of it. His voice was the only one I could hear. I leaned into the door to open it, but to my surprise, it didn't budge. Who locked a multi-person bathroom? I put my ear up against the door to see if I could make out what he was saying, but I could only make out the rise and fall of his tone. He seemed angry. A loud noise startled me, and I fell backwards onto the ground. Paul had slammed a fist against a stall door. The metal was ringing loudly, and the sound echoed through my mind. I heard the door unlock, and Paul stormed out. He startled when he saw me, but quickly recovered his composure and reached a hand down to me. I grabbed it and pull myself up.

"Thanks," I said meekly.

He started to walk away, and I quickly followed.

"Is everything alright?" I asked, praying for a response. He glanced down at me, brow furrowed.

"I can't answer that here," he said and quickly jogged back to the field. Paul brushed past Corbin, causing Corbin to glance in my direction. I saw him break from the group and head towards me. My legs begged for mercy, and I gave in and sat on the slant of the hill. Corbin joined me and we sat in silence.

"You look tired," he offered. I nodded with my eyes closed.

"Where were you today, Corbin?" My own voice sounded slurred and drained of life. He stared back at me blankly.

"Why don't you sleep Amelia? We can talk later." His voice was drawn out, like he was trying too hard to be someone he was not.

I shifted down and lay on my side, my arm curling into a V above my head for a pillow. I was so unbelievably tired and even more lost than that. My brain became a chaotic tangle of thoughts in a skein with too many knots already. "When?" I asked, my voice barely audible.

He shifted down and lay beside me on his back, his hands in his jacket pocket. I could see his breath as it hit the air. "At the party tomorrow."

I barely heard his answer and then the world went blank.

***

I awoke the next morning from a buzzing on my phone. The message was from Kellen.

Don't forget about tonight. 8pm. Be there or BE SQUARE!

I groaned and threw a pillow over my head. The clock came in to focus and eventually the blur of red displayed the time of 10:38 a.m. I shot straight up and grabbed for my phone to message Kellen back.

There was a sixth person that night, Paul - a boy from your soccer team.

It slowly started to dawn on me how horribly unsuccessful I had been during my time at observing things. Maybe I shouldn't be messaging Kellen. Maybe I shouldn't be talking to him at all. I needed to focus, and despite the fact that we had the same common goal, my meetings with Kellen seemed to be less than productive. My grandmother knocked softly on my bedroom door.

"Amelia …" she whispered.

"Yeah." The sound of my voice cracking surprised me. My grandmother stepped into the room. She frowned when she saw me.

"My hair is that bad huh?" I patted my head. She laughed and sat down at the edge of my bed by my legs where she could get a good look at me.

"Something's wrong," she said matter-of-factly. I shook my head 'no,' but she continued to study my face.

"I've known you your entire life, Amelia. I wasn't asking you; I was telling you."

"I have to go to a party tonight," I said, giving up on trying to convince her nothing was wrong. "With a boy who likes me."

She nodded. "You're afraid the same thing will end up happening at this school that did at your last school."

I didn't respond, and she got up from my bed and placed her hand on my cheek, pausing, obviously deep in thought. "I know you're scared, but you have to take your losses and learn from them. I can see the pain twisting inside of you, but you have to fight it, prevent it from breaking who you are. You are important to the world. God gave you an immense amount of compassion and heart for a reason."

She left me to mull over her words. I did nothing but stare at the wall for a good half hour before forcing myself out of my bed to start my day.

***

Because I had slept my morning away, the afternoon came and went quickly. Before I knew it, I was standing in front of my closet doors willing the right outfit to jump out at me. I changed my clothes four times before settling on a pair of skinny jeans, a few layers of tank tops that complimented each other, a belt around my midsection, and a pair of brown knee-high boots. I stared at myself in the mirror as I gave life to my curls. I would blend in at a barn party, but not look like I lived on the farm. I nodded with approval and reminded myself that tonight might be a good opportunity to talk more with Paul and Corbin and maybe, if I was lucky, get a word in with Adam, Taran, and Sam. Find out who that final unnamed person was.

When I arrived at Kellen's house, I sat inside my car for a bit, staring at my surroundings. I was ready for this. I was … about to walk into a house in which a boy to whom I was attracted was alone. My nerves suddenly set fire.

I was not ready for this.

"Deep breaths, Amelia. Deep breaths," I told myself as the panic started to bubble inside of me. I bolted for the door the second I had calmed down, afraid if I gave myself too much time, I'd end up unknowingly driving my car right back out of his driveway and home.

"Kellen …" I called out as I carefully wound down the narrow spiral staircase that led to the basement, paying close attention to my footwork to avoid falling. The last thing I needed to do was to pinball down the stairs.

As he came into view, I noticed he was staring into a mirrored wall, spiking his hair to perfection ever so carefully. When he noticed me in the mirror, he turned to me with an enthusiastic grin.

"Well?" he asked, trying hard to suppress his excitement. I stop to gawk at him from a safe distance. His hair is a shockingly bright red. Like, fire-engine red. I tried to look at it long enough to form an opinion about it, but my eyes got lost in his, and the world started to swirl around me.

I smiled before I could even think to attempt to contain it. Without thought I moved in closer to him. A red streak of hairspray and dye was running down his forehead, so I brought my hand up to wipe it off, and he quickly wrapped his arms around my waist and closed any amount of space that was between us.

"You can't expect me to not take advantage of you being this close to me, can you?" he asked and softly rubbed his nose back and forth against mine, our foreheads pressed together.

I pulled my head back a few inches and glanced up at his hair. "You're crazy," I reply. My mouth suddenly felt extremely dry, and I realized I couldn't feel my body.

A shy grin broke the serenity on his face, and he stepped back.

"Ready?" he asked, sensing my nerves. I nodded in response, afraid that my voice would fail me. He grabbed my hand and led me back up the winding staircase.

When we arrived at the barn, it was already swarming with people. I quickly glanced around for Corbin or Paul, but couldn't find either one of them. Kellen grabbed my hand and pulled me through the crowd – with grace – until we reached the drink table.

"I'm driving," he shouted at me, even though we were only inches apart. The music was so overwhelming I could feel it pulse through my body. I had to focus hard to pick out individual voices. He held out a beer. "Are you drinking?"

I shook my head, and he instead handed me a Diet Coke.

"Want to go outside for a few minutes? So we don't have to shout at each other?" I nodded in response and once more he grabbed my hand and led the way.

Outside of the barn, he leaned against his car and took a long swallow of his soda. I hesitated, but then joined him in leaning against the car.

"So, what was that message about this morning? Paul?" he asked.

"Last night I saw him in my dreams. I didn't realize he was there before." I watched Kellen as I spoke, but his gaze was directed at the ground.

"How'd you know his name?" he asked with suspicion in his voice.

I frowned. Way to pay attention to the important stuff Kellen. "I was paired up with him in math class yesterday." I see relief twitch through his expression and he nods.

"Why are you worried about how I know Paul?"

He kept his eyes focused on a spot on the ground and shifted uncomfortably against the car before finally glancing up at me.

"I talked to Sam yesterday," he said, ignoring my question.

"And?"

"And I don't think he's who we have to worry about. I found out his mom just got a really big promotion at work and despite the facade he puts on, he's pretty straight."

"Straight?"

"He has a 3.9 GPA. I don't think he's ever touched a drug in his life. He kept talking about all these scholarships he's going for."

I nodded. "How the hell did you figure all that out? I thought you never talk to him?"

"I've got my ways," he said with a playful nudge.

"Why did you ask about Paul?" I pressed.

He shoved his hands deep into his pockets and stepped away from his car. He kicked around a few stones and dirt before turning back to me. "Can I show you something?" he queried. I nodded, and he tilted his head towards the barn and started to walk towards it. I followed.

Once we were inside, he glanced around the room and headed toward a hay bale in the corner. He climbed on top of it, adding a few feet to his 5'10" frame and offered a hand to help pull me up. He pointed to a small group of girls on the far right side of the barn.

"See the girl in the red shirt?"

I squinted over at the group and found a girl in a red shirt. He was watching my face, so I tried my hardest to maintain my composure as I studied her. She was slim, but toned and had long, beautiful blond hair. Even from across the room I could make out a pair of shockingly blue eyes. Her red shirt most likely didn't even qualify to be a shirt since it wasn't doing its job of covering her entire midsection. I tugged on the bottom of my tank top, suddenly really aware at how frumpy I probably looked compared to her. She began to laugh with her friends, and I cringed when I noticed everyone within her view was practically drooling over her.

"That's Lainey Petermann. I've had a crush on her since the eighth grade," he whispered into my ear.

I kept my eyes trained on her, afraid of what expression he might see in my face if I looked back at him. I squirmed, but didn't respond. Kellen grabbed my left hand and turned me towards him.

"I've been after her for four terribly long years." I could see the frustration in his face as he said it. "Every time I thought I had a chance, she'd get some boyfriend from another school, and I'd be left waiting for them to break up."

I felt the need to shift, to make space between us, but the hay bale wasn't very big, and I had nowhere to go. He looked back over to Lainey.

"The second week of school she just showed up at my locker one day. She was there to inform me she had broken it off with her boyfriend over the summer. That was all she had to say, but she winked as she walked away from me, leaving me to think she had filled me in on this bit of gossip for a reason."

I could hear my heart beat loudly in my ears. I tried to convince myself I really didn't care and if he wanted to chase a dream that had been four years in the making, I was happy for him.

"She came to me, Amelia. Four years of waiting, and she was practically handing herself to me." He was staring hard into my eyes, enough to cause me to want to jump down off the bale. I hadn't the slightest clue where this story was going, but I didn't like the way my body was reacting to it, and I'd had enough.

"That's great, Kellen; I'm really happy for you. Can I get down?" I slipped my hand from his grasp and turned to jump down, but he grabbed me by the arm. I stared hard at him, feeling my face get red again and suddenly realize I was holding my breath. He leaned towards me, leaving a very small amount of space between us.

"The day you walked into sociology class," he started again, staring so hard into my eyes I could no longer focus on anything but his. "Everything changed. I felt like I found something that I didn't even know I was missing. I was drawn to you, Amelia." The air in my lungs was burning, and I couldn't comprehend the fact that there were more than one hundred people in the room with us. It felt like we were the only ones who existed.

"You can fight me as much as you want, or you could just give in. You could just settle for being my friend, too, but just so you know, we're much more than that. It was never a question in my mind as to whether or not we were going to be together. We are 'us' and no one could ever comprehend how powerful that really is." He then quickly ran his finger down my cheek and turned to jump off of the bale. I looked back out at Lainey, and she glanced up at me, then quickly looked away again with a slight scowl, as if she knew I had taken something she wanted.

"You don't even know anything about me," I shouted out at him as he quickly moved away from where he had left me standing.

He shook his head and turned back to me, stepping towards me to make sure I could hear him. "I don't have to Millie; I can feel it. It's as though I never had a choice. The moment you walked into my life, everything fell into place. The world made more sense, and something deep inside me told me that this," he motioned between us, "wasn't even a choice to be made." He shuffled backward before disappearing into the crowd, leaving me alone to think about what he had said.

It took me a moment before I realized I most likely looked like an idiot standing on top of the bale, hovering over everyone else. The tension and shock was slowly starting to release its grip on me, and I was about to get down from my perch when I heard a commotion by the door. I glanced over to see Corbin entering the barn, Adam in tow. I crouched down a bit so I wouldn't be so noticeable, but stayed on top of the hay bale so I could keep tabs on where they went. Adam swiped someone's drink out of his hand and quickly swallowed it in two gulps. When he handed the guy back his empty cup, the guy lunged at him.

"Who the hell do you think you are?!" a voice growled from the ground before the sickening sound of fist versus flesh rang through my ear drums. I watched as Adam scrambled to his feet, and something metal caught my eye as he moved to adjust his jacket.

A gun. Adam had a gun.

I scrambled to get off of my perch and almost lost my balance in the process.

"Kellen!" I yelled out, and a few people turned towards me with annoyed looks on their faces. I glanced around, but didn't see Kellen anywhere in my immediate surroundings.

"Screw it," I mumbled to myself and started making my way towards Corbin and Adam.

chapter seven

I quickly weaved in and out of small groups, making my way over to Corbin and Adam in record time. It was a benefit of being a petite person. What wasn't a benefit of being petite was that people tended to not hear me approach. I came up behind Adam just as he was bringing his arm back to punch the other boy. His elbow collided with my face, and I fell backwards before realizing what had even happened. My hand flew to cover my eye, and I glanced up to make sure bodies weren't going to start piling up on top of me. Thankfully, my interruption had caused enough of a distraction to give someone time to separate the people involved.

Someone reached down and started to pull me up by my arm. Once I gained my footing, I looked over to see it was Paul. I groaned and grabbed my face.

"I don't think there's any ice here." He glanced around. "I know there isn't any ice here. Come with me." He puts his hand on

fly

my back and guided me out of the way of the fast-growing crowd of observers.

"Let me see your eye, ye of little coordination." He pried my hand from my face and winced.

"What?" I chirp.

"Amelia," he scolded.

"What?" Panic was beginning to rise in my chest.

"Are you sure that you have a date to the dance? Because with your luck, you're going to get trampled." He chuckled a little.

Before I had a chance to respond, I heard a voice behind him.

"She's sure," Kellen said sternly.

Paul froze and stepped off to the side.

"Thanks for your help, Paul," Kellen stated, while examining my right eye, never actually glancing over at him. "I've got it from here."

Paul crossed his arms and nodded to Kellen before walking off without another word.

"You'll be fine. Colorful, but fine," Kellen assured me. Concern flooded his face. "We're going." He grabbed my hand and started to lead me towards the door.

I quickly ripped my hand from his grasp. "Kellen, no." Panic started to rise slowly and spread through me like wildfire. "Trust me, this is the absolute last place I want to be, at a party." I lowered my voice so only he could hear me. "But I came here to get answers, and I'm not leaving without any." I glanced back at Corbin, who was talking to Adam between two piles of hay.

Kellen leaned towards me, arms crossed. The stance reminded me of the one my mother used to take when she was waiting for me to give in to her demands.

"Did you come here for the black eye, too?" he questioned, before brushing past me and getting lost in the crowd. I closed my eyes and shook my head; I didn't need his bullshit right now. I didn't need distraction.

"Soda?"

I looked up and Paul was holding out a diet Coke to me. "You can either drink it or hold it to your face. I fished it from the bottom of the drink barrel." He pointed over to a blue basin bin overflowing with cans that floated in water that had once been ice.

"Thanks," I murmured and held it up to my face.

"You're not drinking?" I asked, glancing down at the Mountain Dew in his hand.

He shook his head. "Shit's stupid."

"Oh, I agree, I just ..." My sentence trailed off as I fumbled for words. Words that didn't cut through me like daggers. Words that wouldn't bring back searing memories and send me into a sobbing mess on the barn floor. He could tell my sudden inability to speak meant there was more to the story.

"My parents are alcoholics," he confessed.

"I'm sorry Paul, I can't even imagine ..."

81

"Yeah, everyone else's parents are all "Be home by eleven p.m.," and at eleven p.m. I have to go hunt mine down and convince them to leave whatever dive bar they've found and convince them to let me drive."

I looked over at him, and I wanted to say something, but the words must have been really stuck in my brain because I couldn't process a single thing to say.

Seeing me struggle, he carried on. "I don't have parents; I have alcoholics. Anyways" – he checked his wrist – "I should get going. Just wanted to make sure you were okay before I left."

I frowned, now more curious about what it was he had been saying on the phone in the restroom that night. Tonight, while I slept, I would have to get in. I had to slip into the bathroom before he did.

"Thanks for the soda," I said, bringing it to my right eye.

Paul walked towards the door, and I turned back to where Corbin and Adam had been, only to see Kellen deep in conversation with them. "Great," I mumbled to myself. I knew Kellen had his self-proclaimed "charm," but he didn't really seem to be on the same page as I was. As a matter of fact, he didn't seem to have much focus at all on the problem at hand. A sudden and heavy weight fell over my chest. Kellen had no idea that Adam had a gun. I quickly walked over to where they were standing.

I grabbed Kellen's arm softly. "Kellen, sweetheart, can you please go get me a soda?"

Kellen blinked in surprise, most likely at the sweet tone of my voice and use of the word "sweetheart."

"You have a soda." He pointed to my face.

"Yeah, this one really isn't for drinking; it's preventing my face from burning with pain." I looked over at Adam, and he grimaced. Kellen rolled his eyes and headed towards the drink table.

"I'm really sorry; I didn't ..." Adam started out. I waved him off.

"You didn't do it on purpose; it's fine," I assure him. I watched him carefully, unsure if I would be able to say something to him about the gun I saw in his waistline. "By the way, I'm Amelia." I grabbed for his hand. "We never really officially met."

"Adam," he replied and gave me a slight smile. He turned towards Corbin. "I'm going out for a smoke. You coming?"

Corbin shook his head. Adam shrugged and walked away.

"You weren't at school today, Corbin," I prodded softly.

"Kellen is really taking a long time to grab that soda," he pointed out as he craned his neck to look for him in the crowd.

"Is everything okay?" I asked him, ignoring his attempt to change the topic.

"Yeah man, I just, I don't see the point." He shrugs as if this was a known fact.

"Of going to school?"

"Yeah, I mean, look at me. I'm not going to college. I'm not yearning to *be* anything." He stared at me, but my expression didn't change. I waited for him to continue.

"Look, Amelia, I love you to death, but I'm not like you. I admire you for working so hard at this school stuff, but it's not for me. My parents don't care one way or another. All they care about is that I keep out of jail and have a job. I got a job. I don't need nothing else. I'm alive. Ya know?"

My face crinkled in confusion. I didn't know. I actually didn't have the slightest clue what he was talking about.

"Is that black eye going to match your homecoming dress?" He pulled the soda from my face. It was his second attempt to change the topic, so I let him.

"Yeah ... I don't really have a dress yet." I shrugged.

"Well then, you'll probably need some help picking one out, eh?"

"Are you offering to go shopping with me? Because, no offense, Corbin, but you don't look like the shopping type."

He shrugged. "You're my girl." He gave me a soft slug on the arm as though I were one of his buddies. "Do you think I'd pass on the opportunity to see you all dressed up?" He briefly gave my outfit a once-over. "And knowing you, you'll probably end up picking out something with long sleeves that falls to your ankles."

My mouth fell open as I took offense, but I closed it once I realized he was probably right. "Alright. Deal," I stated, thinking it'd give me an opportunity to prod a little more into his seemingly bleak future. And maybe ask a question or two about Adam and the other boys.

"Monday then?" he asked.

I nodded. If I remembered correctly from my conversation with Anthony, it was technically my only free day.

"Alright," he said, "I'm going to go and find Adam, make sure he's not getting into any more trouble."

"Corbin?" I needed to know if Corbin was aware that Adam was carrying a gun, but I had no idea how to ask.

"Is Adam, um …" I fumbled with my words. "I came over during the fight because … I saw something in Adam's waistline." I swallowed hard when I saw his face turn stern. He stepped close to me.

"We gotta protect our own, ya know? I wouldn't let anything happen to you, Amelia; don't worry. Sometimes these preppy snots think they can slip away without paying us; they don't fuck around if you got a gun." He stepped back and nodded at me once before walking off.

Paying them for what? My mind flashed back to a catty girl at lunch a few weeks ago. "They're like the drug lords of the town," she had said. *Corbin, what are you getting yourself into?* I set the soda on the hay bale next to me. It was doing a fabulous job of keeping my face numbed from pain, but it was also making it so

I couldn't feel my fingers. Kellen appeared in front of me, eyebrows raised.

"Where's my soda?" I asked him with a smirk on my face.

"Ha ha. I got the hint."

"Oh?" I questioned.

"Yeah, sweetheart, ready to go now?"

The sound of the party started to overwhelm me. If I took the time to stop and think, horrid memories would flood my mind and that was the last thing I wanted. I had come here for answers, for a chance to talk to Corbin, and I got what I needed, for the time being anyway.

"Yeah." I swallowed hard, hoping to keep memory at bay. I wrapped my fingers between his and gave him a tired smile. "Let's go."

He set my hand on his waist and pulled me close to him, sliding his hand up my neck, his fingers sliding through my hair. I rested my head against his chest and could hear, faintly, the beat of his heart. I focused on it for a moment and the rest of the room faded out. For a moment all I heard was the sound of life beating through his warm body. My entire body relaxed in response and for a brief moment I felt so at peace I could fall asleep standing up. I can't remember the last time I felt this serene.

He pulled away and grabbed my hand once more to lead me out of the door. I saw Anthony as I was on my way out, and he sent me a quick wave and winked at me.

"What was that all about?" I inquired when we got into his car.

"Anthony?" he questioned.

"No, before that," I bit out, knowing full well that he knew what I was referring to.

He shrugged. "You needed a hug," he stated, as if it was entirely obvious.

"Oh I did, did I?"

He raised his eyebrows.

"Fine," I said. "I needed a hug. Let's go."

He smiled at the thought of his victory and pulled out of the drive.

The fifteen-minute trip back to Kellen's house was enough to make me realize how drained I was. My body felt heavy and unfamiliar. And to make things worse, my heightened senses were nothing short of really, really annoying. Every little sound and movement became irritating: the sound of the radio, the feel of the bass, the air blowing out of the vents, the way I had to brace myself every time we came to a stop. The only thing I could manage to think about was the way I felt when Kellen was holding me. How had he done that? He made the rest of the world disappear.

"Thank you, I had a good time," I said as he turned the car off in the driveway. I rubbed my face in attempt to wake myself up a bit, completely forgetting about my run in with Adam's elbow. I groaned in pain and hung my head a bit before sliding out of the car.

"Are you alright to drive?" Kellen questioned while making his way around to my side of his car.

"Oh yeah, I'm perfectly fine," I lied.

"Really?" he asked, but it was more of a statement than a question.

I nodded and fished in my purse for my keys. "Crap," I muttered and strode to my car.

"What's wrong?" Kellen asked, still standing by his passenger door.

I pulled on my door handle, but it didn't budge. Awesome. I peered into the car, but didn't see my keys in the ignition where I expected them, nor were they on the seat.

"I can't find my keys," I muttered, too tired to feel any embarrassment.

"Probably because you didn't look in my pocket," he explained as he pulled out a familiar key ring.

"You took my keys?"

"It was in case you got drunk; I didn't want to have to fight you for them," he offered.

"Thanks, but I didn't drink." I held out my hand expecting him to hand them over. He slipped them back into his pocket and started towards his front door.

"Kellen," I said sternly.

"Amelia," he shot back without pausing in his stride. He stopped in the doorway, his back holding the screen door open. "You're tired; come inside, rest a little." He nodded towards the house.

I didn't budge.

"My parents are gone for the night; you can text your grandma and let her know that you'll be home late because you don't want to drive tired. She won't argue with that. Safety first."

I stared at him for a minute. I wanted to be mad because he was, once again, just flat out telling me what to do, what to feel. Even more, I was beginning to realize that, like so many times before, he was right. I was too tired to move, much less stay alert on my drive home. I shivered at the chill in the air. The nip the breeze caused me to feel sent my feet towards the door.

"Millie." Kellen nodded to me as I walked past him and into the house.

I stood awkwardly in the foyer, not really knowing where I was supposed to go. Kellen closed and locked the door behind him and headed into the kitchen. I followed, plunking my purse onto the counter and settling in on a stool.

"Cocoa or cider?" he asked while rummaging through the cabinets, presumably for a mug.

When I didn't answer, he offered, "Warm milk?" with a disgusted look on his face. "Gross."

fly

"Cider," I replied, knowing that the answer *nothing* wasn't an option.

"Ugh, we're fresh out," he noted with a wince. When I didn't say anything, he stepped over to the tall cupboard. "I'm kidding. Eesh, tough crowd."

A few microwave beeps later Kellen placed a mug of hot cider in front of me. "So,how was your night?"

"I'm not any closer to figuring stuff out, if that's what you're asking." I took a drink out of my mug to avoid talking, immediately regretting it. The sugar in the cup wasn't going to wake me up, but the burning did a fine job of that. My eyes immediately started to water, but if Kellen noticed, he didn't say anything. He probably was trying to make me feel as comfortable as possible, not pointing out obvious things like, "Oh hey, that cider I just microwaved is hot." Damn him. Damn him for being so unbelievably perfect. My mind started to wander, but I caught it and tried to steer it in a different direction.

"I saw you talking to Corbin and Adam. What was that all about?" I asked.

"I asked them about the fight," he said coolly before carefully sucking the top layer of marshmallows out of his cocoa.

"And?"

"And ..." He looked over at me and squinted his eyes a bit as if he were deciding whether or not to tell me the rest. "And I'll fill you in on a need-to-know basis. Until then, you don't need to

90

know." He finished off his drink in a few gulps and set his cup in the sink. I stared back at him, bewildered. I was on a need-to-know basis. Did he not understand how extremely important it was that I knew every detail? I didn't have a lot of time left. I had seven days, not seven months.

He walked past me, brushing his finger along the bridge of my nose on his way out of the kitchen.

"I'll go find you a long-sleeved shirt to change into; meet me downstairs when you're done," he said as he left the room and headed for the spiral staircase.

I stared down at my mug of cider, feeling ten times more alert than I had when I walked through the door. I took one more drink from my mug and poured the rest down the drain. I was fine to drive home now, and I needed to go to bed. I would just go and demand Kellen give me back my keys and head home. I'd recite the alphabet backwards and walk a straight line with my finger pressed to the tip of my nose if he wanted me to.

I started to make my way down the winding staircase. Whose bright idea was it to put this stupid thing here anyway? One wrong move, and you'd be tangled up in a mess of metal bars that were supposed to prevent you from falling. As I descended the last curve, I noticed Kellen standing at the bottom of the steps, blocking me from going any further. He had an orange long-sleeved shirt draped over his right shoulder.

"I'm fine to drive home now," I proclaimed, my face never breaking from his stern gaze.

"Oh?" he inquired. "Must've given you the mug laced with NoDoz."

"I'm serious, Kellen." My heart started to beat a bit harder in my chest, and I couldn't tell if it was because I was frustrated or because Kellen was less than a foot away from me. For the first time since we'd met, I was literally face-to-face with him. Because he was trapping me on the last step, we were the same height. He stared at me for a moment before taking my keys out of his pocket. I made a move to grab them, but he quickly slipped his hand behind his back.

"One thing, before you go," he said.

I stared at him, waiting for his next words, afraid of what my voice would sound like if I spoke. I was trying to be mad, to make a point, but my knees were starting to fail me. I wasn't able to stand this close to him without feeling a strong desire to lessen any space between us.

"I did as you asked me to; I think you owe me that kiss." He pointed to his cheek.

I wanted to argue with him, but my brain was too muddled to remember the exact conditions for his "deserved kiss." He brought my keys from behind his back and dangled them between us. I told myself to get the keys, give him a peck on the cheek, and go, simple as that. But I hesitated, visualizing my plan to flee, as if it served as a sure fire way to succeed.

I reached for my keys, but when I leaned in to kiss him on the cheek before running up the stairs, my lips came into contact with his instead. I hadn't considered one slight move of his head would change the entire game plan. I melted at the feel of his soft lips against mine, and without thinking I grabbed a fist-full of his shirt and pulled him in closer, my body completely surrendering to every connection it made with his. I wasn't thinking about how angry I was at him or how much I needed to be at home right now preparing for bed; the world just crumbled away, any small speck of thought vanishing like it never even existed at all.

When I started to lose my balance, Kellen grabbed hold of my shoulders and stepped backwards holding my keys up in one hand and his orange shirt in the other. Still void of thought, I grabbed for the shirt and followed him towards his bedroom.

"If this makes you uncomfortable in any way, let me know," he said with his hands up as if he were under arrest. "I'll keep my hands to myself. Unless you ask otherwise, of course." He turned to head through his doorway, and his movement caused a waft of his cologne to fill the air around me. I felt my legs buckle at the thought of the serenity his hug had caused earlier. I followed, wondering to myself if it were possible to make this last forever. When I entered his room, I slipped off all but one tank top slip and wrestled with the opening to his orange, long- sleeved tee. I made sure to breathe in every ounce of his scent as I slipped it over my head. He was lying on his bed, hands tucked behind his head, watching me closely, as though I might make a break for it at any second. I inched onto the bed next to him and softly ran my hand over his chest. My hand immediately stopped when I reached a bump. He grabbed my fingers hand and held them in his.

"What's that?" I asked, not sure if he were wearing some sort of necklace.

"It's nothing," he replied and kissed me on the forehead. I closed my eyes and slowly breathed him in as deeply as humanly possible, my brain grabbing at his scent and storing away bits and pieces of everything that made him Kellen.

chapter eight

I awoke to the screeching of my alarm at four a.m. Sleeping next to Kellen had put me in a sleep deep enough that I didn't even have the chance to dream. I had missed my chance to find out what it was Paul was saying in the bathrooms that night. In the dark I scrambled for my phone, the source of the alarm. I glanced over at Kellen who hadn't budged.

I reached down for my mess of tank tops and belt but couldn't remember where I had thrown them. I didn't want to wake Kellen by turning on the light. I couldn't chance him glancing at me with pleading eyes, willing me back into his warm bed.

Once I was home, I slipped off my jeans and, out of habit, dug my hand in every pocket before throwing them in the wash. In my back left pocket, I came up with a wad of folded cash surrounding a small white piece of paper. Not remembering what it was, I unfolded it. A phone number was scribbled on it: it was

Paul's. I set the paper on my nightstand, making a mental note to check in with him in the morning. I crawled over to my bed and tried hard to focus on the night of the game, hoping I had one more chance to dream since it was my second time going to sleep. I didn't have Kellen's warm body and beating heart next to me, so I doubted I would sleep too soundly to dream. I closed my eyes and cleared all thought except for the men's bathroom at the soccer field.

To my surprise, it worked. When I opened my eyes, I was standing on top of the hill right outside of the bathroom door, and Paul was fast approaching. I quickly scrambled inside and crouched in the end stall. "Please don't come into the last stall," I mumbled to myself as I heard him barge inside and lock the door behind him.

"What do you want, Michael; I'm at my game!" I heard him yell into his cell. I watched him through the crack by the stall door as he paced back and forth.

"Slow down, slow down. Why were they mad at you?" his voice softened a bit.

"Okay … uh huh …" He was nodding along with his confirmations, and I could hear someone yammering on the other end of the phone, talking in a fast panic.

"You didn't STOP them?!" he yelled. It startled me, and I almost fell off of my crouch on the toilet seat.

He slammed his hand on the stall door, but thankfully, I was still braced from my last surprise. "Where are they?" he bellowed. Within moments I heard him hang up the phone and curse under his breath. I heard the door open and close, but I waited a few moments before I exited the stall in which I was hiding. My phone started to jingle softly, and I scrambled to pull it out of my pocket. One new message. Crap, what time was it? "Wake up," I told myself sternly. With that, my eyes flew open, and the first thing I saw was the blinking green light on my phone, indicating I had a message.

I squinted my eyes, bracing myself for an overpowering bright light. The text message was from Kellen.

You left some clothes at my house.

I cringed. Crap, I hope his mom didn't find them and yell at him. *I'm sorry,* I answered.

Come upstairs and get them, he replied.

Confusion washed over my face, and I glanced at the clock. It was nine-thirty. Had he not noticed I left?

I'm not at your house … I said, confused. Was this wishful thinking on his part?

Nor am I, he replied and added a wink emoticon.

I shot straight up and immediately brushed my hands through my hair. He wasn't. He couldn't be. How the hell did he even know where I lived? No, he wouldn't. I heard some clamoring around in the kitchen, and I snuck out of my bedroom

97

and into the bathroom to quickly brush my teeth and wet my hair. I quickly threw my hair in a braid and assessed my appearance in the mirror. What the hell was I doing? He probably wasn't even upstairs. It was probably just a stupid Kellen joke. When I exited the bathroom and started up the stairs, I could hear my grandmother's laughter followed by … Kellen's. I stopped halfway up the stairs and buried my face in my hands. Whatever happened to asking to come to someone's house, or I don't know, getting invited over?

"There she is!" my grandmother exclaimed as I became visible. She was standing next to the stove watching over three separate pans and had a large grin on her face. Her silver hair was pulled back in a clip, but half of it had fallen out around her face, as usual.

"Amelia, Kellen just stopped over to apologize for your late homecoming last night." She smiled over at Kellen who was sitting at the kitchen counter with convincing charm written all over his face.

I cleared my throat in the hope Kellen would take the hint and talk to me privately, but he didn't move from his seat. "Hey Kellen?" I asked. "Can I talk to you a second, over here?" I nodded towards the other side of the kitchen and looked over at my grandma who was busy analyzing her food.

When we were out of view, I wasted no time in attacking him. "WHAT are you doing?" I quietly shrieked

He looked at me confused. "Granmillie is making us breakfast," he replied as if it's totally normal.

"Granmillie? Kellen, her name is Bernadette," I said in annoyance. I wasn't amused.

"I know, but I told her about how I call you Millie and she wasn't against me using it in her name too. She actually thought it was adorable." A smirk crawled across his face.

"Ugh!"

He looked behind us and, seeing no one, stepped a bit closer. I froze at his action, but didn't drop the scowl from my face. He tipped my chin up to him and smiled.

"What?" I took a step back, fearing I had toothpaste or soap left on my face.

"Your eyes are even more gorgeous without all that make-up on them." He said before he turned to walk back into the kitchen.

I rolled my eyes, even though he didn't see me do so, but I could feel myself blush at the compliment.

After breakfast I thanked Kellen for coming over, hoping he would get the hint that it was probably time for him to go. My grandmother started to clear the table.

"We're going for a walk," Kellen said as he leaned in my direction.

"We?"

"Yeah, just you and me. I need to talk to you." He folded his arms, and I noticed his expression turn serious. "Do you want to take a shower first?" he asked.

I glanced over at my grandmother who was busy loading the dishwasher. I shook my head. "Not for a walk. Just let me go change."

I paused before heading up the stairs and grabbed my phone and the white piece of paper with Paul's number written on it. I quickly typed in a text and saved his number on my phone.

Thanks for your help last night. Hope everything is ok? - Amelia

I wanted to know what it was he was talking about on the phone in the bathrooms. Whatever it was, it seemed urgent, and I could hear a spark of fear in his voice that I hadn't yet heard. After all, he still couldn't be ruled out as the person needing help.

When I came back upstairs after getting ready, my grandmother and Kellen seemed to be deep in conversation in the kitchen. They both grew quiet at my appearance.

"Ready?" I asked Kellen.

He turned back to my grandmother and gently placed a hand on hers. "It was a pleasure meeting you, Granmillie. I hope to see you again soon. Thank you for breakfast; it was amazing." He flashed a bright smile at her. I watched her smile back at him, her eyes alit with joy.

fly

"Thank you for stopping by, Kellen." She stepped back, and Kellen started towards me.

"Shall we?" He held an arm out towards the door, and I waved goodbye to my grandma. "I'll be back soon," I told her.

We drove out to a small park and parked in the deserted parking lot. I raised my eyebrows.

"There's a trail." Kellen pointed and got out of the car. He came around to my side of the vehicle and grabbed hold of my hand. "Millie?" He tugged on my arm a bit, and I followed.

We walked for a few minutes before I finally broke the silence. "Is this about what Corbin and Adam told you?" I asked him. He shook his head and didn't take his eyes off of the ground.

We walked for a few more minutes before he paused at a fallen tree. "Come, sit," he told me, nodding toward the tree. We sat down, and he examined our intertwined hands. I noticed that his expression remained grim.

"Amelia," he started. I wince at the use of my full name. When he did, it usually meant serious conversation was to follow. "Why did you move to your grandma's house?" he asked me softly.

The question startled me, and my face froze; my mouth opened to start a sentence but nothing came out. Deafening silence fell over us. He just looked over at me with genuine concern.

"What happened?" he questioned softly. I quickly shook my head as though doing so would rewind time and un-ask the question he had just put to me. I wasn't ready to tell him the story that occurred in my Guardianship, the one that my brain constantly begged me to forget. All that was left was a sinking feeling of loss. "I can't," I murmured, still shaking my head. He said nothing in response, but quickly placed our free hands together and squeezed tightly. My head stopped shaking, and I glanced down at our entangled hands.

"This is the way it's supposed to be," I thought to myself.

"My last Guardianship was related to a boy named Derek," I started. "He was in my class, had been since the beginning of middle school. He was this tall, awkward kid who kept to himself and stayed at the back of the classroom. I usually found myself sitting somewhere around him, and even though he didn't ever volunteer answers out loud, he was as smart as they come." I kept my eyes concentrated on Kellen and took a deep breath, afraid I wouldn't have the strength to tell him the whole story. My heart grew heavy with sadness, but I continued.

"One day when we were leaving math class, a shudder ripped through me. I took a second to glance around the room, but luckily, there weren't many people who hadn't already run out. The teacher called out my name immediately after I felt the shudder, and I caught a glimpse of Derek as he was leaving. A stupid jock knocked him into the doorway, and all of his books fell to the ground. I couldn't follow him because my math teacher wanted to talk to me about my failing grade. She suggested a tutor and mentioned Derek was the only person in the class with a perfect grade. She had already talked to him about tutoring me. The whole thing just kind of fell into my hands and said, "Here I am!" It was no secret that Derek was a prime target for the jocks' amusement, and it didn't take long to figure out how much it was dragging him down." I swallowed hard.

"All he needed was a friend." My voice choked on my words. "What everyone else didn't know was how funny he could be, how intently he listened when you spoke, how he knew every high school football stat related to the two years we had been there. The jocks were complete assholes to him, but he still went to every single game. I started inviting him to my lunch table and to the pregame parties. It wasn't long before everyone fell in love with him." I felt a tear run down my face. I hadn't even realized I was crying.

"One night, before one of the playoff games, one of the players invited Derek to watch the game from the sidelines. One of the water boys had called ahead to let them know he was too sick to make it. He came running to me, eyes wild, barely even able to speak through his excitement." I paused, my heart clenching at the thought of the latter half of the story, the part that was still untold.

"His life flashed before my eyes. I saw what would have happened had I not introduced the real him to the rest of the class. He had written a suicide note and had a plan to swallow a bottle of his mom's pills. He had even done the research to make sure it would lead to death. He didn't want to be alive. Every day I hung out with him, he had hesitated to carry through with his plans and this final day? The day of the game, had completely changed his mind. He felt like he belonged. He did belong."

Kellen cleared his throat before speaking. "You saved his life with hardly any effort. I don't see how that's bad, Millie."

I started to shake my head frantically. "When the game ended, the crowd went wild with excitement. Everyone in the stands was jumping up and down waving their arms. It was then that it happened, a second shudder. I wasn't sure what it meant since it had only been a few hours before I that I had witnessed the flash of "what would have been." I knew I was successful at my mission. After the shudder I glanced down at the field and saw the quarterback, Warren, talking to Derek but I thought nothing of it at the time. Derek looked happy." My breath sped up, and the words started to tumble out of my mouth at a faster pace.

"I ignored the second shudder. I was too worried about rushing off to a party one of the players, Rob, was hosting at his house. All I was worried about was catching Rob's eye and impressing my friends. Halfway through the party I noticed Derek was playing beer pong with Warren. I didn't even know he had come to the party, and I didn't make an effort to go over and say hello. I was too worried about impressing a stupid boy."

More tears ran down my face, and I choked out a small sob. Kellen rubbed my hand, snapping me back to reality for a brief moment. My sobbing subsided, and I stared through him without blinking, my eyes glazed over.

"I never went and said hello to Derek; if I had, I would've noticed he was wasted. I would've taken his keys or offered him a ride home." Kellen winced, his face twisting into sorrow, guessing what my next words would be.

"He wrapped his car around a tree on his way home from the party. He was killed instantly. I failed. He needed my help, and I failed him."

Kellen gave me a moment before speaking. "You didn't give him the alcohol, Amelia," he said softly. "It wasn't your fault."

"I know," I offered through a stifled sob. "But if I had just talked to him, I would've known."

"That's why you're being so stubborn at McHenry, isn't it?" he prodded. "You're afraid having friends will get in the way again? That's why you're being so stubborn with me."

"After that night I was visited by the Powers while I slept. They warned me that failed Guardianship gave the Devil the upper hand. They told me the price they paid for allowing me to save lives was that they couldn't check what the Devil was capable of doing." My voice shook as I spoke. "They told me if I failed again the Devil would be able to …" I shut my eyes, unable to watch his reaction.

fly

I took a deep breath and started again. "The Advocates are failed Guardians, Kellen. Guardians who failed their mission more than twice. They said it was like the story of Job from the Bible. That the Devil seeped in through your pain and suffering of loss and took hold of your moral soul. He replaced it with darkness, and the Powers, no matter how hard they try, can't pull you back out."

Kellen pulled his hands from mine and rubbed his face a few times before running his fingers through his hair. "It's not going to happen, Amelia," he stated sternly, with confidence. He inched towards me and cupped my jaw in his hands. "I will not let anything happen to you, I promise. We'll figure this out."

"Then you need to tell me what's going on with Adam and Corbin!" I begged.

He pressed his lips into a straight line and shook his head. "My number one goal is to keep you safe. I'm not doing that if I tell you what they're up to. I promise you I'll tell you if I think you need to know. You have to trust me." He grabbed for my hand and held it to his heart. "Do you trust me, Amelia?"

I could feel his heart beating hard under his chest. He was scared. I wanted to trust him; I wanted so badly to give into him and let him be the one to wash away all of my pain and fear. But I didn't deserve it and more importantly, he didn't deserve the burden of me.

My eyes shifted to the right of my hand. The pressure of my hand against his chest was causing a small bulge to appear under his shirt. He noticed where my eyes had fallen and quickly pulled my hand away, shifting backwards an inch.

"Tell me what that is," I nodded my head towards his chest. He had avoided the question last night, but I had been too tired to think much of it.

His face filled with panic, and he took a deep breath.

"You want me to trust you? Give me a reason to," I urged him.

He slipped his hand behind his neck and unhooked a metal chain I hadn't even noticed was there. He scooted closer to me and carefully fastened the chain around my neck. I picked up the circular pendant off of my chest and squinted at the small writing. In the center of the medal, a robed man was kneeling on one knee, his hands outstretched to the sky. Around the man the words *Saint Peregrine, Pray For Us* were inscribed.

Kellen nodded at the medal. "I got that a year ago. I want you to have it. I want you to have a constant reminder that I'm here and that you're always here." He grabbed my hand once more and placed it on his heart. He pulled my hand back off of his chest and squeezed it hard. I could see his mind working furiously, trying to perfect what he was about to say next.

My mind roiled with confusion. The necklace wasn't the cause of the bulge in his shirt; it had been too small. And what did Saint Peregrine represent? I knew people who wore Saint

Christopher metals, but I had never really looked into the separate meanings of the saints.

"The bump on my chest," Kellen started and then had to clear his throat. His eyes stayed focused on our hands as he nervously fidgeted with my fingers. "It's a Medi-Port," he said and took a moment before looking up at me. My expression remained focused on him, not changing at his words. He knew instantly that I had no idea what that meant.

"It's a catheter," he said softly, "a way for them to easily administer a chemo treatment straight through to my heart."

His words sliced through my entire being, freezing me into shock and horror.

When he looked back up at me, my eyes were pleading. Just make this go away. I don't want to feel like this anymore.

He stood and pulled me up to stand in front of him. A weak smile spread across his face, and he shook his head when I opened my mouth to speak. He gently placed his hands on either side of my face and pulled me into a long kiss that threatened to rob me of my ability to stand. I wanted to run far away from here and take Kellen with me. I wanted to curse a God that would do this to him, who would threaten to rob the world of such a beautiful soul, but within seconds, the only thing I could see was blank space because Kellen – in every small touch, every breath, every scent – made the two of us the only people in existence.

chapter nine

When we got back to the car, I noticed I had left my phone sitting on the dash, the green light blinking rapidly. Kellen immediately put music on after starting the car and started nodding his head with the beat. With all that was unloaded in the last half hour, he seemed oddly at peace. I carefully watched him for a minute, making sure he hadn't just been deep in thought with words shifting in anticipation of being spoken out loud, but he said nothing.

I hit the power button to display my phone screen and saw that I had four new messages, all from Paul. I had almost forgotten I had messaged him before we had left for our walk.

The first message was a pleasant response to my earlier text which thanked him for helping me at the barn party.

No problem, any time.

The second was in response to the second half of my initial message, asking if he was okay. It had come a few minutes after the first.

Everything isn't ok ...

The third showed hesitation, as if he wasn't sure he was allowed to continue without my prompt.

I never ended up finding my parents last night ... and they still aren't home.

I glanced over at Kellen's dash; it was just after noon. The fourth had come through just before I got into the car, an entire half hour after the third.

Can you meet me for coffee? I don't have anyone else to talk to

You could never actually pinpoint the tone of someone's words through reading them, but I felt a sense of urgency and desperation in Paul's text. I quickly texted him back.

Sure thing, time/place?

He must have had his phone right in front of him because he responded immediately.

I'm already at the coffee shop on 9th Ave. I had to get out of my house. I'll be here for a bit, no rush. And don't feel obligated to come.

"Kellen?" I asked warily.

"Hmm?" he questioned. His eyes stayed on the road, but he slipped his hand over to my leg and gave it a small squeeze right above my knee.

"Can you drop me off somewhere?" my voice emerged, smothered in guilt.

"Yeah, where do you need to go?"

"The coffee shop on …" I look down at my phone "… ninth." I responded.

"Hot date?" he inquired.

My face reddened, and I gave him a coy smile.

"Who's at the coffee shop?" he asked, eyebrows raised. I could tell he was surprised at my silence.

"Paul. He needs to talk to me." I glanced down at my cell phone and quickly added, "We still haven't ruled him out as needing our help."

"Paul? Need help? With what?" Kellen's voice was more stern than usual, and even though he tried to contain his facial response, I could see the muscles in his jaw clench.

"I'm not sure yet," I lied.

I didn't intend to keep Kellen in the dark if I really thought Paul was in need of our help, but I wasn't sure yet, and I didn't want to go around spilling all of Paul's deepest secrets for no reason.

Kellen pulled in front of the coffee shop and parked directly in front of the bay windows. I glanced inside and saw Paul sitting at the coffee bar facing the street.

"Need me to come with?" he asked hopefully.

I shook my head and gave him an apologetic smile. He leaned in closer to me, his elbow resting on the center console. He hooked his finger around his medal, which was hanging around my neck, and softly tugged me forward.

"Millie? One favor?" His voice was barely above a whisper.

"Hmm?"

His lips brushed over mine, and my breath momentarily escaped me. His mouth was cool and filled my mine with the sweet taste of spearmint. When he pulled away from me, I absentmindedly ran my tongue over my lower lip.

"What was that?" I demanded, knowing full well that Paul could see straight into Kellen's car from his perch at the window.

"It was me, saying goodbye," he replied with a mischievous smile. "Call me if you need me? I'll be around town."

I grabbed at the medal on my neck and ran it back and forth along the chain.

"Mmhmm," I said as I got out of the car. Kellen had this ridiculous way of causing my brain to forget how to say words.

I stepped on to the sidewalk and glanced up at Paul. His face was buried in his hands, his hair sticking out at unnatural angles. I took a deep breath and headed inside. I ordered a tall coffee at the counter and spent a minute adding tons of cream and sugar. Paul hadn't even turned to look at me. Maybe he hadn't even seen us pull up in front of the bay window. I slowly walked over to him and took the seat beside him.

His eyes were glazed over, and he didn't even flinch when I sat down.

"Paul?" I said softly.

A few seconds later, he slowly turned towards me. His unkempt appearance tells me that he hasn't gotten much sleep, if any at all.

"Hi, Amelia," he said after clearing his throat. "Thanks for coming." He offered a weary smile.

"What's going on?" I queried. My body was fully turned towards him, letting him know he had my full attention.

He again rubbed his hands over his face and took a long draught of his coffee. He shook his head. "Everything is just a huge God-damned mess. I'm just tired. SO tired. I have to spend every day not only looking after my three siblings, but also my parents who don't ever seem to know if they're coming or going. I mean, do they even realize they have responsibilities? My mom can't even remember half of the conversations she has with me. Two nights ago, I told her I was going to kidnap the kids in the middle of the night while she slept and take them somewhere where they wouldn't have to deal with her bullshit anymore. The next day, when she woke up, she hadn't even remembered seeing me the night before. She started going off about how I wasn't home in a timely manner." He traced his eyebrows with his fingertips, hanging his head to the counter. I saw his leg start to bounce violently. I gently set my hand on his leg, bringing it to a stop. He finally glanced over at me, and I couldn't tell if he'd been crying or if he was just that emotionally and physically exhausted.

"What happened last night?" I asked.

"I left the party to go out and look around for them, see where they were, and get a good idea about whether or not I needed to get them home. I couldn't find them. They weren't at any of their usual spots, and when I started to go inside the bar to ask the bartenders for help, they not only wouldn't help me, but they were suspicious about the fact that I was even there. They thought I was just using some lame excuse to be inside the bar or buy myself time to blend into the crowd. The more I drove around looking, the more I hoped I'd run into them so I could call nine-one-one and report a drunken driver. I gave up at four a.m. and went home to sleep for a while, but I couldn't. When the kids woke up, I made them breakfast and settled the two younger ones in with some cartoons. I filled in Michael – he's fifteen – on what was going on. Told him I needed to get out of the house and clear my head. With all of the rage that I was feeling, not to mention the exhaustion, I wasn't sure what would happen if they walked through the door."

I thought back to the night of Kellen's soccer game last Thursday. His conversation in the bathroom had been so one-sided I hadn't the slightest clue what it was about. I took a stab in the dark and asked, "Does stuff like this happen a lot?"

I watched him carefully as he thought about his answer. His eyes darted around as though he was searching for words. "No," he said, "it's not always this bad. I mean, my "not that bad" is worse than other people's bad because they're drunk every single day. I'm just so tired." He seemed unable to find the right words. He picked up his coffee, but his cup was empty, so he threw it in the trash can next to him.

"Last Thursday ..." he started. I perked up at his words. Was it really that easy? He tapped his fingers on the counter and drew a large breath. "Last Thursday during my game, my brother Michael kept calling me. I mean, I had twenty-five calls over the span of an hour. It was getting excessive but soccer is the only time I ever get to just forget everything else exists, you know? He finally texted me nine-one-one, so I ran up to the bathrooms after I was pulled out of the game for the last time. I knew they wouldn't throw me back in with only a few minutes left." He squinted at me, deep in thought. "I think that's the night I ran into you, right?"

"Literally." I smiled at him, embarrassment surely showing through my wince.

"I called Michael back, intent on reaming him out for disturbing me during the only 'me time' I get, but the panic in his

115

tone changed my mind. My parents had left the house drunk that night. They had gotten into a small fight with Michael and Anna, who is thirteen. The two of them had tried to express how unfair it was that they never got to be kids and do whatever they wanted to because they always had to look after our youngest sibling, Joshua. He's only five and can prove to be a bit rambunctious. He gets into everything and you're constantly having to keep an eye on him. My parents surprised Michael by saying they understood what he was saying and they'd fix it. They left that night, for the bars, and took Josh with them. Michael would have run after them, even though he doesn't have a license, but he didn't have access to a vehicle." He finished his story and looked over at me.

"The bars would let them bring him inside?" I asked, irate at his parents for being so irresponsible.

"It was only seven-thirty; the bars around here consider that the dinner crowd and wouldn't have forced them to take Joshua home until ten. By then they'd be way-beyond capable of driving. So I rushed straight over to Sulley's Tavern, took Josh, and went home. I let him sleep in my room that night. As a matter of fact, they all did. Everyone was afraid of them coming home in a drunken rage and raising hell." He shook his head, a look of disgust scrawled across his face. "They didn't say a single thing to us Friday morning. It was as though it had never happened."

Paul's cell went off, and he quickly jumped off of his seat. "I gotta go," he said to me quickly, running his hand rapidly through his hair.

"Are you going to be okay? Do you want me to come along?" I stood as well, but he shook his head.

"Thanks for listening, Amelia, I really needed to ... I just really needed it. I owe you one. See you Monday, in math?" He was already halfway out of the door, so I nodded and waved him off.

I sat back down and slowly sipped my coffee. Paul's home life was a mess, and Corbin was heading down a bad path if he wasn't even intending to graduate from high school. Adam carried a gun on him, and there seemed to be something else, something a lot bigger going on with Corbin and his friends.

How was I ever going to figure this out?

chapter ten

I hung around the coffee shop for a few minutes after Paul left. I pulled out the folded sheet of paper with my list of the people from the soccer game and finished my coffee while mulling it over. I scribbled Paul's name on the back with a question mark. I didn't need notes for him. The memory of his home life was unfortunately seared into my brain. I had watched him carefully while he spoke, and he looked truly troubled. If he had been lying as some sort of ploy, then he deserved an Emmy for his performance. I was deep in thought when I heard someone slip into the seat next to me.

I didn't need to even look over to know it was Kellen.

"Kellen," I said, my voice pleading. "I need to know what you were talking to Corbin and Adam about."

He shook his head without hesitation. My heart sank in frustration.

"Do you see this?" I shook my paper in his face. "I haven't a clue where to start. You know how much is on the line; why won't you just tell me?" My voice couldn't have sounded more desperate, but there was no reason to hide my frustration. I was starting to run out of time, and the heaviness of everything I had learned in the last seventy-two hours was starting to weigh me down. I wanted to be angry at Kellen. I wanted to blame him for the road blocks he placed in my way, but no matter how hard I tried to prevent it, my heart ached when I looked at him. I was fairly certain I was falling in love with him. The weirdest thing about it was it didn't feel like a choice. Like he had said before, it felt as though it was a simple fact of the world. The grass was green, the sky was blue, and I was in love with Kellen.

I stood, and my heart picked up its pace as I found myself battling between what I wanted to say with what I needed to say.

"I'm leaving." I shoved the paper back inside my purse.

"Okay." He rose and started to walk with me.

"I'm walking home," I said sternly, not looking back at him for fear I'd break down crying if I saw anything less than a smile on his face.

"Don't you want a ride?" he asked. I didn't respond or pause.

"It's a couple of miles home, Amelia." I could feel him mere inches behind me as he spoke. I stopped at the door, pausing a moment to gather my strength. Unsure of what my voice would sound like, I simply nodded and walked out. I needed him to understand how important this was to me. How much I needed to know everything he knew.

I knew he was concerned about protecting me, but keeping information from me when my soul was on the line wasn't protection. The harder I tried to pay attention to everything and everyone around me, the more confused I became. I was concentrating so hard that everyone I came across seemed to need intervention. The only person I could be sure didn't need help was Kellen.

As a matter of fact, Kellen was supposed to be helping me. Helping, not hindering. The thought of Kellen sent my stomach tumbling. I thought back to our conversation in the woods and absentmindedly grabbed for the necklace on my neck. I saw flashes of the night of the barn party, the way he stood so close and how my body hummed to life whenever he was near. I also had flashes back to the moment when he first kissed me on the staircase and how that kiss had made my world fade to nothing.

I paused, noticing the sudden familiarity of the streets leading up to my house, but my thoughts remained firmly fixed on Kellen. My mind was taking time to remember the solid beat of his heart, when my head was resting on his chest, the fact that it was the only thing I could hear, even though the rest of the room was pierced with music and laughter. Deep in thought, I was surprised when I realized I had turned the corner to my road. It was strange how a few miles felt like a few short blocks because I had so much on my mind.

I took a deep breath as I grabbed for the door handle on the front door. I would spend the afternoon doing my homework and pushing everything else back to the farthest reaches of my mind, at least until tomorrow.

Hopefully.

When I got into the house, I threw my cell phone in my room and headed upstairs with a backpack full of books, hoping to get lost in the life of a shark, the topic of my essay. I worked on the paper until dinner and then stopped to help my grandmother prepare the meal. After dinner, I decided to snuggle up on the couch with a blanket and cup of hot cider afterwards to watch Sunday night programming on TV. The combination of being cozy, watching emotional drama, and having an emotionally exhausting day caused me to slip into a light sleep without realizing I was even tired at all.

I awoke when I felt the light touch of someone brushing the hair from my face and softly saying my name. As my eyes struggled to focus, the soft edges of Kellen's face came into view. My stomach sank at the thought of him. I was angry at him, but at the same time, I wanted to grab him by the shirt and pull him next to me on the couch. I wanted to curl up against the warmth of his body and disappear into the blank space that seemed to come whenever we were together.

I wanted the world to disappear.

I sat up and pulled the blanket around me, hoping to trick my body into warmth and comfort without him.

"What are you doing here Kellen?" I asked, in as harsh a manner as I could muster. "What time is it?" I turned to glance over the couch at the stove clock, but the numbers were only a red blur.

"It's nine-thiry," he answered. "Granmillie let me in; she said to tell you she was heading off to bed."

I stared back at him, sleep still making any reactions I wanted to display hazy.

"You weren't answering my calls." His brow furrowed. "I was worried."

I felt a small lump rise in my throat. I swallowed hard, willing the thought of our conversation in the woods earlier today out of my mind. However, the thought won out, and I slowly reached my hand out to his chest, trailing my fingers along his Medi-Port and pressing my palm against his chest when I reached his heart. His heartbeat thumped against my skin, steady at first, and then the rhythm picked up a bit. I looked up from our hands, and he quickly put his hand up against mine.

"Millie?" he questioned softly. I could feel my own heart starting to pick up its pace at the sound of his voice, however soft it had been. I looked down at our hands, my eyes widening in response.

"Amelia," he said, a bit louder. A hint of a question mixed with a plea played in the sound of his voice saying my name.

"Hmm?"

He reached up to my face with his other hand and gently tipped my chin up, our eyes locking. When he knew he had my complete attention, his spoke again, with sincerity. "I promise …" He pressed my hand harder against his chest; his heart felt like it might tear its way through his chest. "… I will never do anything to hurt you."

The lump found its way back to my throat and I couldn't swallow. I trusted him. There was no way someone could lie with that much promise and truth in his voice. He put his hand to my face and gently kissed me on the forehead before heading towards the door.

"Goodnight, Millie. See you at school," he said before closing the door behind him.

After a few minutes, I made my way down to my bedroom. I started to arrange the pillows on my bed when an orange shirt caught my eye. I should've given it back to him when he stopped over. I glanced over at my phone, the green light blinking, showing I had messages. I grabbed it and scrolled through missed calls and messages from Kellen. He hadn't messaged me since he left.

I have your shirt, I sent him.

His response was immediate. *I wasn't worried about it, and you can keep it if it makes you think of me.*

I rolled my eyes at my phone and crawled into bed. I pulled his shirt closer and, out of curiosity, held it up to my face. Despite the fact I was the last one to wear it, it smelled like a mixture of his cologne and the hairspray he used to spike his hair. My heart skipped a beat as the smell brought back a rush of memory. To my surprise, a small, choking sob escaped me as I remembered running my fingers over his port. Kellen had cancer. Cancer. Tears rolled down my face faster than I could wipe them away. I inched closer to a row of pillows that lay beside me. Every muscle in my body was suddenly aching for Kellen to be lying there with me. I was being so childish; I could've asked him downstairs. I could've asked him to lie with me until I fell asleep. I could be tucked up against him, the world melting away. Instead I was cold and alone, and tears wouldn't stop collecting on my pillow case.

I must have eventually fallen asleep because when I opened my eyes, I was standing on the soccer field at McHenry, in the same spot I had witnessed Kellen's shudder the night of the game. I whirled around to look for any signs of life, but no one was with me.

"Kellen?" I called out, hoping my thoughts of him as I drifted into sleep had somehow allowed me to talk to him in my dreams. "Kellen!" I yelled once more, but my voice just echoed back at me. I shivered, my body suddenly really aware of how alone I was and how badly I wanted to be in Kellen's embrace. I glanced up at the bleachers and saw a boy sitting in the far left corner. The red hood of his sweatshirt was casting a shadow over his face, so I couldn't see who he was.

I froze, suddenly fearing I might have an idea why I was here.

"Hello?" I said, this time with less urgency. The boy got up and walked over to the press box and quickly let himself inside.

The speakers facing the field let out a mess of static, and I quickly started to jog up the bleachers.

A voice then broke through the speakers, urgent and rushed, "Jackson takes the handoff, cuts left, breaks a tackle, and now he's running down the sidelines. He's at the forty, the thirty, the twenty; can he go all the way? Touchdown Northwest Eagles, Steven Jackson number twelve!"

I paused at the mention of my old high school football team, but I opened the door to the press box, and the boy in the red hood swiveled his chair towards me.

"Amelia Thompson." A thin boy with shaggy dark hair and glasses too big for his face was grinning widely at me, swiveling left and right in his chair, his hands tucked away in the pocket of his sweatshirt.

"Derek?" I managed to choke out. Then my legs started to wobble, and he quickly rolled a chair towards me.

"Easy, Amelia." His face became serious for a brief second until I was sitting down again, then it stretched back into a wide grin, showing a display of uneven teeth.

"How are you?" he asked with eagerness as he leaned towards me, listening intently.

I blinked. "What?"

He leaned back and took a minute to read me. "What's going on, Amelia?" The smile had faded from his face. I glanced out over the field, and it remained empty.

Now I was swiveling back and forth in my chair, nervously staring at Derek. How could he even talk to me right now? How could he stand to be near me? I had failed to save his life; he should hate me.

"Hey, what happened that night, it wasn't your fault." He seemed to be reading my mind. "Tell me, what's going on? You look … you look like you need someone to talk to. I'm listening."

I stared back at him, refusing to speak, refusing to believe that he was here to help me when I had failed him.

"Amelia." The corner of his mouth twitched for a brief second, as though a thought were dancing across his lips. "How about I start? I know who you are. I know you're a Guardian, and I know you were assigned to help me. I don't blame you for what happened. If you need me to say it a hundred times, I will, but I honestly don't think we have the time for that, so you'll have to take my word for it. Do you know how happy I was in the days before I died? I went from wanting to kill myself to feeling on top of the world. Never in my life have I ever felt that rush of …" He balled his hands into fists, and I could see happiness rumble through his body as he tried to find the words. "I never felt so alive Amelia! You gave me life." He brought his fists up to his heart.

His face fell, and I could see him moving on to the next thought. He brought his arm down onto the armrest of the chair and tapped the palm of his hand against it before continuing. "There was an Advocate working against you, but you already knew that. What you don't know is they know who you are. They know who you have to save. It isn't hard for them to wiggle their way into your life and use the pureness of your heart to distract you."

My body temperature rose at his confession. That wasn't fair. It wasn't fair for them to have an advantage over me, over the Guardians. We were blind, and they had all the answers, before the questions had even been asked.

"Do you know who was working against me when I was trying to save you?" I finally asked in a low, quivery voice.

He nodded. "You're not going to like it, though. Are you sure you want to know?"

I nodded back at him quickly, leaning in to be sure I heard his answer.

"It was Rob. He couldn't be directly involved with my death, which was why he introduced me to the biggest drunk on the team. He also knew enough to keep you distracted. He knew if he batted his eyes at you and kept himself just out of reach you'd have to put in more effort … try a bit harder to get his attention." Derek winced at his own words.

"He told Warren to hang out with you that night because he knew he'd get you drunk?" I asked, wanting to be sure that I had heard him right.

He nodded. "Played his part, but indirectly, without getting his hands dirty."

"This isn't fair Derek! I don't have a cheat sheet! I have no idea who I'm supposed to save; I have no idea who the Advocate is! I'm on the side of good; why don't I get clues and hints like they do?" My voice came out a shrieking mess.

"Amelia …" Derek brought my arms back down to my lap. "… you do have an insight; you're just not listening to it."

"What?" I asked, confused.

He picked my hand up off of my lap and brought it to my heart. "You're not listening to this, Amelia," he said. I looked at him quizzically, so he continued. "Your senses are heightened. You have the ability to pick up sound." He tapped a finger to my ear. "You have the ability to pick up certain smells." He brought his hand down and tapped his finger against my nose and then held it up as if to say 'wait.' "Which also entails listening to the memory that binds to smell." He touched the top of my head and then brought his free hand down to join the other two pressed against my heart. "Most importantly, learn to listen to this. You know that flutter or that gut feeling you get? It's for a reason.

You're supposed to listen to it, trust it. Pay close attention to all of these things, and you'll figure it out."

I stared at him, not sure if I should thank him for the tips or hate myself for not realizing any of that earlier. Did Kellen know these things? Was I really that negligent? Derek shook his head at my thoughts.

"Don't go there," he warned. "Don't beat yourself up. You've been handed a tough case, that whole listening with your heart thing came naturally to you for all of the other cases. This time, it's harder because it's happening with complete strangers, and you have so much heart that you worry about all of them."

He stood and stretched, glancing out over the field. He turned back to me, wide grin back in place. "I have to go, and you have to wake up now."

I wanted to beg him to stay, but I didn't know how quickly my alarm clock would rip me from my time with him.

"Thank you," I said. My heart hammered loudly in my chest as I stood and pulled him close for a hug.

"You can do this," he whispered into my ear. I closed my eyes and nodded into his shoulder. When I opened my eyes again, I was hugging my body pillow. My alarm went off before I had time to curse the morning, and I rolled out of bed.

"I can do this," I whispered to myself before rushing to the bathroom to get ready for school.

chapter eleven

When I arrived at school, Kellen was waiting for me by my locker, his head hanging. I couldn't tell if he was about to tell me bad news or if he was afraid that I was angry with him.

"Good morning?" I said slowly. His green eyes burned through me, begging.

"You're just going to loiter around my locker looking all emo?" I asked as I unloaded my backpack and gathered my things for my first-hour class.

A wry smile danced on his lips. "I just didn't know if you hated me right now," he replied.

My heart sank. I didn't think it'd be possible to hate Kellen. The forces of nature wouldn't allow it. I was definitely frustrated with him, but that wasn't going to keep me from him. I had learned my lesson last night from the agony of curling up to a pillow, willing it to turn into his warm, soft body.

"Can we get dinner tonight? My treat," he said. He had perked up a bit since I had first approached. I loved the enthusiasm that had spread like fire lighting his face, and I cringed, knowing I had to tell him 'no.'

"I can't," I stated as I shut my locker and leaned against its door next to him. "I'm going homecoming dress shopping tonight with Corbin."

"Why the hell does Corbin get to go with you?" His response had come too quickly, and I could tell that he wasn't able to censor his anger.

I shrugged. "He asked."

"Isn't that, I don't know, weird?" I could see a flicker in his eyes. Jealousy?

"Corbin was the first friend I made when I transferred here. I didn't necessarily want to be his friend, and I actually tried really hard not to be, you know, because I didn't want any friends. But he was really persistent, and eventually I just had to give in to him because he wouldn't leave me alone. After a while, I realized there was no harm in having one friend. He seemed harmless. He grew up with five sisters so he kind of took on that brotherly role with me. I actually didn't mind it at all seeing as I have no siblings. He asked if I had a dress when we were at the barn party and told me he'd help because he didn't trust me to pick something out that didn't cover every inch of my body."

I could understand jealousy, but there was also something called trust. I couldn't tell if Kellen trusted me or if he simply didn't think he was allowed to voice his opinion. Corbin's mother was Hispanic, and in her world family came first. A person had to protect and take care of family. Corbin had, more than once, referred to me as hermanita, which meant little sister in Spanish. I felt safe with him, and even if he didn't appear to be the safest-looking person, I knew he had good intentions and my best interests at heart.

Kellen nodded at my last statement, tacitly agreeing with Corbin. "Smart guy," he offered. "Does he know you're going to the dance with me?"

He seemed extra vulnerable this morning, and it was tugging on my heartstrings. I just wanted to bury my face in the crook of his neck and breathe in the safety and warmth that he offered. I wanted to forget everything was a mess and melt into his world. I couldn't think of the words needed to ease his worried mind. Couldn't think of a way to tell him that, in a way, he was the only person I really saw at all. The bell rang, ripping me from my thoughts. I started towards the English classroom, and Kellen followed.

"Uh, yeah, he knows. He makes it perfectly clear I'm like a sister to him. I promise you, Kellen, he doesn't have a hidden agenda," I replied. We stopped in front of the door, and Kellen quickly kissed my forehead before running off to his first-hour class before the bell rang. I watched him disappear into the crowd before going inside.

In my second-hour study hall, I was relieved to see Corbin waiting for me at our usual table.

"Hey, what time did you want to go shopping?" he asked as I sat down. I immediately smiled at the thought of his remembering our shopping date. I didn't honestly think he'd forget, but somewhere deep down inside, I was scared that since I was actually looking forward to it, he'd forget or make other plans.

"I don't know, six? We could grab a quick bite to eat on the way," I suggested.

"Alright, sounds good, but you gotta pick me up at my house. I ain't got a car, ya know."

"I can do that," I said with a nod.

"Hey, Amelia?" he asked, his voice lowering with the sound of the second bell.

"Yeah?" I whispered back, leaning towards him so we wouldn't get yelled at for talking.

"Do your math," he said in a scolding manner, pointing at the math text that was pushed furthest away from me.

I rolled my eyes at him and swapped out my pile of notebooks for my homework. I opened to a blank page and tapped my pencil a few times against the paper. My mind was wandering to my dream the night before with Derek. I had been trying very diligently to keep the memory of the dream as far out of reach as I could because it made my stomach flip every time I pictured Derek's face.

Derek's voice finally broke through the barrier of my thoughts, loud and clear: *He also knew enough to keep you distracted. He knew if he batted his eyes at you and kept himself just out of reach you'd have to put in more effort... try a bit harder to get his attention.*

There wasn't anything I could remember about Rob that would have warned me about his cruel intentions. Everything I remembered about him made me think he was simply fun loving and warm hearted. There didn't seem to be a dark and brooding side, no black cloud hovering overhead. My stomach twisted sharply as I glanced up at Corbin. Could he be working against me? My pulse picked up a beat before I heard Derek's words again, this time when he had placed my hand against my heart: *And most importantly, learn to listen to this,* he had said.

I closed my eyes and sat back in my chair. The room was silent, but I could hear the sounds that people usually didn't even notice like the clicking of a pen against paper, a bouncing leg, the turning of a page, someone chewing gum too forcefully. Sitting next to Corbin, I felt nothing but warmth and adoration. I opened my eyes, and he was staring at me with raised brows pointing to my math book. I rolled my eyes at him and started to scribble down my first math problem. For now, I felt safe saying he wasn't the Advocate. But that assumed Derek was right and I was listening to my intuition properly.

When I got to lunch that day, I sat down at Kellen and Anthony's table and picked apart my sandwich as I waited for Kellen to show up. After the lunch line had closed, I leaned towards Anthony. "Where's Kellen?" I asked.

"He had a doctor's appointment." He reached into his sweatshirt pocket and pulled out a shiny blue package. A Rice Krispie Treat slid to a halt in front of me. "Said to give this to you. He'll be back by sociology; don't worry."

"Is he alright?" I felt a sudden panic bubbling up inside of me.

He nodded his head as he quickly finished chewing his food. "Yeah, just a checkup. He has them a lot for testing and whatever. I think he has to start another chemo round in a few weeks."

I pushed my sandwich towards the center of the table and opened the Rice Krispie Treat. I wondered why Kellen hadn't mentioned anything to me this morning. More importantly, did I have a right to know such things? I suddenly realized how out of place I felt at the table without Kellen there. Sure, I was friends with Anthony, but he was busy talking to the other people at the table. I sat quietly and listened to Scott and Matt speak in foreign-sounding geek speak. The only thing I could understand was that one of them was building a computer. Anthony seemed to be deep in conversation with Michelle about decorating for the homecoming dance, and I was afraid they'd notice me sitting quietly and start asking me my opinion on things. I was not the creative kind; they would be better off asking someone who was colorblind for their opinion on the color scheme.

I sat back in my chair and closed my eyes. I thought I'd take a stab at Derek's suggestions regarding my heightened hearing and try to differentiate sounds in the noisy cafeteria. The mixture of chatter, clanking of silverware against trays, and crunching of wrappers was overwhelming. I cringed at the way the overbearing noise made my body tense up, on high alert. I was about to open my eyes when, for a brief second, the room went silent. My eyes flew open at the piercing quiet, and I looked around, but everyone was still chatting: I just couldn't hear them. The silence was only for a split second before I heard the sound of a spoon clanking against the tile floor, and it echoed through my ears. I had just enough time to turn towards the sound and pinpoint where it had come from before the sound of the entire room came flooding back. I immediately stood, and I glanced up to see who had dropped the spoon, only to find Adam and Corbin sitting on either side of where it had dropped. Unfortunately, the bell rang right after I stood up.

"Whoa, looks like we've got ourselves a psychic," Anthony said as he got up and grabbed his tray off of the table. When I turned back to look at Corbin, he and Adam had already walked away from the table and were headed towards the hall. The sound of the spoon hitting the ground had most certainly not been the only sound in the room, so there had to have been a reason that it was the only thing I heard at the time. The Powers had to be telling me one of those two boys was either my mission or the Advocate. I needed to figure out which one, and thankfully, I'd be able to throw in some questions during my night with Corbin.

Later when I arrived in sociology class, I immediately noticed Kellen's absence.

"I thought you said he'd be back," I demanded of Anthony. He shrugged without looking up from his book.

I sat down at my desk and could feel my nerves start to dance. I didn't like that Kellen wasn't here. I didn't like that Anthony had expected him back, but he wasn't. Normally I'd chalk it up to how a normal doctor office visit could sometimes take way longer than expected. Sometimes it took sitting in the office for a good twenty minutes before the doctor would even stroll in. They were busy places, and it was impossible to expect prompt timing out of them. Patients were at their mercy. This would have been a valid excuse to calm my nerves, but Kellen was at the doctor for his cancer, and cancer was nothing to mess around with.

The second bell rang, and the teacher started to call for our attention at the board, but I only heard a blur of sound. My mind was going wild with "what if's," and those hypotheticals were all I could seem to concentrate on. Ten minutes into the class, the door latch slowly opened, and I saw Kellen's wild, red, spiky hair poke through the door.

"Mr. Anders, welcome to class," the teacher greeted him. Kellen walked over to her and handed her a slip of paper, presumably his pass for being late.

He slipped into his seat and started to arrange his books on his desk, ripping a piece of paper from his notebook. My nerves, one by one, started to calm. The teacher resumed her lecture and a piece of paper slipped onto my desk from behind me.

Did you miss me? Kellen had written, followed by a winking-smile emoticon.

My face reddened at the answer that immediately popped into my head. Yes, I missed him, but that was stupid. He had only been away at lunch and for the first ten minutes of class. How absolutely ridiculous would it be to admit to that?

I wrote back, *Nah, Anthony keeps good company. I barely noticed you were gone. How was your appointment?* and twisted my arm behind my back for him to grab the sheet of paper from me. I didn't want to draw the attention of the teacher by actually turning my entire body to face Kellen.

I tapped my eraser on my notebook, impatiently waiting for Kellen's response. The pink tip bounced happily off the paper, as if bouncing was its only purpose. I hadn't the slightest clue of what the lecture was about, and I was sure I'd regret it later, but I could always bug Anthony for his notes. He seemed a little overeager when he was taking them.

The sheet of paper slipped back on my desk. Kellen had written *Yeah, bad news …* My body went numb at those three words, but I read on. *…apparently I have cancer.* I shook my head and shoved the page under my notebook. If he was going to be an ass, I wasn't going to try and have a serious conversation with him. I guess I really didn't expect him to tell me the every detail of why he had been there in the first place, but I was concerned. I didn't even want to think about my world without him in it, even if I had only known him for a few weeks.

Another piece of paper was placed on my desk.

Sorry, really bad joke. It was just blood work. It took so long because I stopped to get a burger on my way back to school. I wasn't in a hurry to get back. Hey, are you missing anything?

Yeah, I thought, *my dignity*. I looked up at the teacher and saw that she had just started a sentence on the board, so I took the opportunity to glance back at Kellen with a questioning expression. He held up his hands and wiggled his fingers. I glanced down at my hands. What on Earth was he talking about?

I scribbled a question mark on the page and put it back onto his desk. When it came back to me, he had written *Only 2 rings?*

I glanced down at my hand. I normally wore a stack of three thin glass rings on my left hand. Only the pink and clear one were on right now because I had misplaced the blue one. How did he notice that? I turned back to him, but he motioned for me to give him back the piece of paper. I, once more, slipped it behind my back and waited for him to return it.

You left it at my house, he wrote, *and when you didn't call me freaking out about if you had left it there, I figured you didn't really care too much about it. I may or may not be currently wearing it. (That depends on whether or not you need it back.)*

His fingers were much larger than mine, and I hadn't seen it on him when he wiggled his fingers at me, but maybe I wasn't looking closely enough. The sound of the teacher's voice broke through my thoughts.

"I want you to get into small groups and discuss the impact of poverty on the individual, the community, and society as a whole. I'll put up white poster paper and have you write what your group comes up with. You've got fifteen minutes. Go."

I winced. I hadn't been paying attention this whole time, and I hadn't had the opportunity to read the chapter before class like we had been asked to. I felt Kellen tap me on the shoulder, so I turned towards him. Now that the teacher was done talking, it was safe to break from my usual forward position.

"We can work with Anthony; he was paying attention," Kellen told me. I saw Anthony shake his head in partial annoyance, knowing he was the only one who would have any answers. When I looked back at Kellen, I noticed he was wearing a thin black rope around his neck.

"New necklace?" I asked.

He grinned. "Yeah, I gave my old one to some girl."

He ran his finger along the necklace and pulled it out of his shirt to show me. To my surprise, each side of the rope was tied to the blue ring that was missing from the group that I usually wore.

"Do you need it back?" he asked.

I shook my head, unable to form words.

"Good, it makes me think of you. Not that I have to be reminded, because I most certainly don't, but I like having it. Besides, you have mine; it's only fair you give me something in return." He turned backwards to face Anthony. "I can write the answers on the paper if you want me to," he offered.

"Absolutely not. We want people to be able to read it, Kellen. Give the marker to Amelia." As usual, he hadn't even looked up from his notebook as he spoke.

"Here you go, Millie. I'll read them off to you," Kellen said as he handed me a red Sharpie and grabbed Anthony's notebook off of his desk.

We got up and walked over to the white piece of paper. My world was a mess, but when Kellen was right beside me, no matter what disasters threatened to rip through our worlds, I felt like I was right where I belonged.

chapter twelve

I swung by Corbin's house to pick him up at six that night. I spent the hours after school pacing my kitchen trying to think of a valid excuse to cancel my dress-shopping date. It wasn't about Corbin; it was about the fact I couldn't remember the last time I had bought a dress, and I hadn't the slightest clue about what I was doing. In the end, my memory of Kellen's hopeful eyes when he had asked me to the dance and the fact that I could use my hours with Corbin to ask more questions about his conversation with Kellen won out. If there was one person whom I knew would be patient and understanding with me about my lack of "girly-ness," it'd be Corbin.

Thankfully, he was waiting outside of his house when I pulled up, so I didn't have to deal with the awkwardness of going up to the door and asking for him.

"Hermanita." He smiled at me. "You ready for this?" he asked as he softly punched me in the upper arm.

"Nope," I said matter-of-factly and shifted into drive. He laughed a little and rested his elbow on the open window of his door. He played with the small tuft of hair on his chin absentmindedly, appearing to be deep in thought.

"Where do you want to eat?" I asked, not wanting to interrupt his thoughts but needing a direction in which to drive.

He smiled at me slowly. "We're not eating first. Drive to the Plaza," he demanded as if I had no other choice.

"But I'm ..." I started out, but he cut me off with the wave of a hand.

"If we eat first you'll not only complain about things not fitting right, but you'll have less energy because you'll be all sleepy and sluggish from being full. If we dress-shop first, you'll be more likely to make a decision because you're hungry and you have something to look forward to afterwards."

I said nothing and stared at the road as I drove. I didn't think I'd be able to argue myself out of his plans for the evening, but I wished I would've grabbed a snack on the way out of the door earlier.

"Corbin?" I asked gently. He looked over at me, eyebrows raised, ready to play defense against my words.

"Can you open my glove box? I need something to tide me over until dinner." I smiled at him.

"You keep snacks in the glove box," he said. It was as more of a statement than a question. Then he chuckled to himself as he tossed the Rice Krispie Treat onto my lap.

We arrived at the strip mall, which consisted of a large string of stores, all of which had to be entered from the outside.

"What color are you looking for?" Corbin asked as we slowly made our way towards the door.

"Huh?" My face twisted into a confused mess. "Am I supposed to know?" I asked, my voice sounding rushed and panicked.

He chuckled a little and shook his head at me. "No, I just thought you had a favorite color or knew what color looked best on you."

I shoved my hands deep into my zip-up jacket.

"Hey," he said while stepping closer to me with each stride. He put an arm behind me and squeezed my shoulder, shaking me up a bit. "This will be fun, I promise. And you'll look amazing either way." He gave me a sly smile, and I couldn't prevent myself from smiling back.

After we walked into the dress section of the first large store that we saw, I headed straight for the racks and started to rifle through them. It might have seemed to an outsider that I was a "normal girl," excited to find the perfect dress for a dance I spent hours of my day squealing over. The truth was I just wanted this to be over with, and I really wanted to get some food.

My phone buzzed in my pocket so I reached down for it. I pushed the power button to reveal that I had a new message from Kellen.

Whatever you find, you'll look gorgeous. Call me when you're done?

A smile crept over my face as I replied with only the letters *ok.*

"Amelia."

I looked up to see Corbin standing in the aisle between departments. His voice had sounded stern, and I immediately slid my phone into my back pocket and threw my hands up in defense. "Sorry. Dresses." I nodded.

"Amelia, you're in the woman's section."

I gave him a confused look. "Obviously. That's where you find the dresses," I shot back.

His body shook with a chuckle he tried to hold under his breath, but a small sound had escaped. He brought his hand to his mouth balled into a fist and coughed his way through his laugh as he stared at the floor and simply pointed to our left. I followed his finger straight to a section of rack upon rack of short, glistening dresses. I glanced back at the rack behind me and realized that most of the dresses were the sort that I'd seen my mother wear.

I could feel my face grow red. "I …" I stammered a bit, flustered. "Ugh!" I started over to the racks of short, colorful dresses and glanced back to see a smug smile on Corbin's face as he trailed behind me. I spent quite a while circling the racks before finding Corbin. "Alright, next store," I said.

"Oh?" His brow raised in question.

"Yeah, they don't have my size in the ones I liked." I had to stifle my own shock at how good the lie that fell from my mouth was.

"And what size is that?" he asked.

I stared back at him, and he pointed towards the dressing room. "You go that way and find a room. I will bring you a few to try on. We're not leaving until you establish some sort of preference." I frowned at him, but marched over to the dressing rooms anyway.

I sat on the bench in the changing room until a dress came flying over the top of the door. It was dark purple with even darker purple swirls and designs creating a pattern throughout the dress. A black sash tied underneath the bust. I glanced at the length and my stomach dropped. I quickly opened the door. Corbin was sitting on a chair outside of the dressing room.

"Problem?" he asked.

"Yeah, it's too short." I held it back out to him.

"Try it on," he urged.

"No, you don't understand, I hate my legs."

"Amelia, it's the length of ninety per cent of the dresses out there. Just try it on," he insisted, his voice now scolding.

I glanced back at the dress and grimaced. I closed the door and was about to start changing when I got an idea. I whipped the door back open.

"How about … if I try on the dresses you bring me, no matter how much I really don't want to – and trust me, I REALLY don't want to – you'll tell me what is going on with you and Adam and whoever else." The nerves in my body stopped dancing.

"Okay?" he said.

I nodded, and not wanting him to change his mind, I quickly closed my door. I slipped the dress on and stared at myself in the mirror for a minute. I looked like a girl. I felt a little naked. I yanked on the hair tie that was holding my long curls in a messy ponytail. They spilled onto my shoulders and somehow made me look a little less seductive.

"Amelia." Corbin said from his perch outside my door. I took a deep breath and opened my door.

"Well?" he asked.

"What?! I'm showing it to you!"

"What do you think?" he asked.

"I think I look like I might be going on a date with Barney." I absentmindedly tugged on the bottom of the dress, trying to make it longer.

He closed his eyes and smiled a bit, pinching the bridge of his nose between his fingers. He grabbed another dress off of the chair next to him and folded it onto his lap.

"Adam is mixed up with some …" He looked around quickly, surveying how many people were within earshot of us. No one was around. "Adam is buying pills from someone at school. He was testing out the supply to see if what he was getting was legit. It was, and the person who he was buying from offered him a discounted rate if he bought in large quantity. Adam agreed to it because he realized that if he bought in bulk, he could then sell and not only make money from it, but get his own stash for nothing." Corbin glanced up at me and I waited for the rest of the story. He had paused as though there were more, but instead he held out the dress that had been on his lap.

"To be continued," he said waving the dress to make it dance.

I quickly grabbed it and closed the door behind me. The dress that he had handed me was black and had a punk feeling to it. The bottom half had a few layers of mesh on the outside, the kind you usually found on the underside of the dress to make the skirt poof. I put it on and only quickly glanced at the mirror before opening the door and stepping out.

"Nineteen ninety called. They want this back so I won't be able to wear it Saturday," I said before he could ask.

"Continue," I urged him.

He grabbed another dress off of the stack and started talking. "Adam put in his order for his massive stash of …" He trailed off, and we watched a woman walk in and slip behind a door on the other side of the room. Corbin waited until he heard her rummaging around before he continued. "… massive stash of muffins. But this time, unlike all the other times, the person he was buying from was demanding the money before he gave him any muffins. The baker said the amount of muffins Adam was ordering cost more than what the baker had on him on a normal basis. There was going to be a three-day lag between payment and delivery. So Adam paid the baker seven days ago."

The woman in the other dressing room swore under her breath, causing us both to look over at her. Corbin's eyes widened, and he pursed his lips as if he knew what that had meant. He held out the next dress without looking over at me. I grabbed it and once more headed into the room. The dress that he had handed me was different shades of blue and fell to my ankles. It only draped over one shoulder and sat snug only in one thick strip around my ribcage. I grabbed a handful of the skirt so that I wouldn't trip over it and opened the door.

"Corbin, this looks like a toga," I said with a hint of annoyance in my voice.

"Well, maybe you should have had an opinion when we were looking at the dresses in the first place. It's all part of a greater plan, Amelia; don't worry." He glanced down the hall to make sure no one else had snuck into the room.

"It's been seven days, and the baker still hasn't brought the muffins for Adam. Adam fronted a lot of money, like more than most of us probably have in our bank accounts. The baker keeps saying he doesn't want to bring it to school and he keeps having all this "stuff come up" so their plans to meet up keep falling through. What the baker doesn't know is Adam is no one to mess with. Adam is the exact opposite of someone you want to mess with. He showed up at the barn party that night looking for the baker so that he could put the fear of God into him."

He held out another dress, and I grabbed it from him. "Corbin?" I asked before receding to my room.

"Yeah, Amelia?"

"Will you eventually tell me who the baker is?" I asked.

He shooed me into the dressing room with a flick of his wrist without answering my question. I slipped on the dress, but this time paused before walking out. I stared into the mirror, shocked by what I saw. The dress was a tight strapless piece that was covered in silver sequins. A sheer black lace hugged the dress right below the chest and fell down the front, , still showing the sequins underneath, and then to my ankles in the back. I felt gorgeous, and I didn't know what to do with the feeling.

I opened the door and stepped out, feeling the sheer fabric dance behind me as if I had my own personal regal court.

Corbin raised his eyebrows and shifted forward in his seat.

"Continue with the story," I urged.

"No witty comment about this one?" he asked with a smug smile on his face.

I shook my head and crossed my arms, hoping to look commanding.

He leaned back and smirked at me. "I know you saw the gun at the party; that's what I mean by "you don't mess with Adam." He's fearless, he has nothing to lose. The baker can't keep messing with him or something really bad is going to happen. Obviously he can't go to authorities and say, 'Hey this man took my money and didn't give me my muffins,' so he'll take matters into his own hands and it's not going to end well. When you ran into us at the game the other night, Taran was trying to convince Adam to approach it differently, but he wouldn't budge."

"Do you know what he's planning to do?" I asked.

Corbin only stared back at me.

"Is this what Kellen knows about? What he refused to tell me? Were you talking to him about it at the barn party?" My questions were falling out of my mouth without thought as panic began to rise. I was closer to the truth, but not close enough.

"Kellen knows," he said as he held out another dress.

I felt a grip on my heart as I grabbed it from his hand. My other hand absentmindedly went to the necklace that rested on my chest, and I slid the pendant from left to right along the chain.

I slipped on the dress and sat down on the bench in dressing room. It was littered with the dresses I had tried on. I rubbed the bottoms of my palms back and forth on my forehead. Did I feel anything 'off' when I was with Corbin? No. Did I hear anything odd? No. But then again, I hadn't been listening to anything but his story. Maybe I wasn't focusing. I buried my head in my hands and took a deep breath. I stood up and walked out of the room without even glancing at myself in the mirror. When I exited the room, Corbin stood up from his seat on the chair.

"Amelia," he said.

"What?" I asked, suddenly worried that I had forgotten a piece of the dress and was standing there half nude.

"Did you look at yourself?" he asked, his eyes wide.

I rushed back into the dressing room and saw what he had been gaping at. I was wearing a silver dress that fell mid-thigh. It was held up by thin straps and rested on my chest in a way that was both modest and a little bit flirty. The top part of the dress was smooth satin silver with a sheer, lighter silver fabric bunched over it. A gray sash went from underneath my chest to my hips, hugging my ribs and showing off the true shape of my midsection. Right at the hip, the dress puffed out a bit; the sheer gray rested softly on the satin fabric. A very detailed design drawn in silver glitter decorated the bottom half of the dress from the bottom up to my midriff. It was gorgeous and it made my skin tone glow. I nodded in approval as Corbin watched my reaction in the reflection of the mirror. I closed the door and changed back into my clothes.

I didn't ask Corbin more about Adam and the baker until we were seated at the diner waiting for our dinner to be served. I tucked my hands underneath my legs and leaned forward a bit to be sure that no one was listening.

"Corbin. Who's the baker?" I asked quietly.

He took a long drag of his soda, but I could still see the drop in his face, as though he was hoping I'd forget. I continued to lean forward and listened as attentively as possible, as if I only had this one opportunity to hear his answer.

"It's Paul, Amelia," he quietly said.

chapter thirteen

Our food arrived in the moments of silence that had followed his words. He continued to stare down at his drink, and I slipped my hands beneath the table and clamped them together, squeezing my fingers so hard the pain became a distraction from the thoughts racing through my head. When our food arrived, I pushed it around a bit, unable to force my appetite to come back to me. I think Corbin knew I needed to process what he had told me because he let the silence continue the entire way home.

I thought back to all of the times I've talked to Paul, thought of his unease, the worried look on his face. I always attributed it to the problems he had at home, but they could've been brought on by the trouble he had gotten himself into also. My mind flashed back to the day I had Kellen drop me off to meet Paul for coffee. At the mention of Paul's name, Kellen's face had gone hard and serious. I had assumed it was jealousy, but now I knew what Kellen knew then. He was probably torn between letting me have coffee with Paul and telling me about the drug deal in order to prevent me from having coffee with him. I had thought the cold, hard expression that came at the mention of Paul's name was born of jealousy, but now I know it wasn't. Or at least, not entirely.

Disappointment sat on my chest hard and heavy and threatened to smother me. The lump in my throat was practically throbbing with pain, warning me that if I tried to swallow, it might close up entirely. At what point does the pain of disappointment trump the prospect of being happy? At what point do you consciously make a decision to stop putting yourself through hell for the chance that you might one day be happy? I'd never in my life wanted so badly to snap my fingers and be home and in my bed praying for sleep to replace all heartache and confusion. I didn't want to be awake, allowing thoughts to run wild through my mind, eating up every ounce of energy I never even had in the first place.

When I pulled into my driveway after dropping Corbin off, I got a glimpse of someone sitting on the front stoop; my headlights made him visible for a split second. My heart started to beat rapidly, and just when I thought that I couldn't be any more miserable, the weight of the night started to spread throughout my entire body. I turned off my car and sat in silence for a moment before getting out. I wasn't ready for Kellen yet. I hadn't had time to process how I felt about all of this. I hadn't had time to prepare my words, to make sure they got my point across. And quite honestly, I didn't know if I could even walk at that moment without my body deceiving me and trembling the entire time. He was standing at the corner of garage, letting me know he was there, but not eagerly approaching me as he normally would. I grabbed my dress out of the back seat and started towards the door that led to the house.

"Amelia," he said loudly, a pleading statement. I froze for a moment. It was as though he already knew what I found out and that I had every reason to be angry with him. I just stood in the glow of the garage light and stared at him. I didn't have words, but I did know I had things to say and that the longer I put it off, the more it was going to eat at me, distract me from my mission.

He slowly walked toward me and grabbed the bag with the dress in it out of my hands.

"Can we talk?" he asked in a meek, soft voice. I didn't speak or nod, just continued into the house knowing he was trailing after me. The foyer light was on, but it appeared my grandmother had retired for the night. Part of me was relieved because I didn't want to have to try to put on a happy-go-lucky face for her before running off to another room to talk to Kellen. I just looked around and then waved him on to follow me downstairs. He followed me into my room and hung the dress on the bar in the closet. I still didn't know what to say to him, so I panicked and grabbed my pajamas off of the bed and went out to the bathroom to change. My feet felt like they weighed a thousand pounds, and it took all I had not to just curl up on the bathroom floor and pass out.

I came back to my room wearing my pajamas, teeth brushed, hair tied back into a braid, make-up washed clean from my face. I normally would hesitate at washing my face until after Kellen left, not wanting him to see me so raw, but I figured if the discussion got heated I'd more than likely start crying, and I didn't want to have to deal with the messy, awkward task of wiping away make-up stained tears.

He was slumped on my bed, fidgeting with his hands, head tipped downward as if he was about to confess his deepest secrets. He looked up when I closed my door, and I noticed the color had drained from his face, leaving a reddish purple tint around his eyes. My hand automatically went to my necklace, and my stomach sank. He reached out for my hand and I gave it to him. He grabbed on tightly and pulled me towards him quickly, immediately wrapping his arms around my midsection and gently placing his ear against my chest. I had to set my hands on his shoulders in order to keep from falling, and I could feel him burning up. His muscles were tense, and I could feel the rapid beat of his heart rumble throughout his body. His hair wasn't in its normal spikes, but instead was soft and moist with sweat, but I ran a hand through it anyway and let my palm rest on the side of his face. After a few minutes of standing like this in silence, I could feel the tension melting out of him at every slow, steady beat of my heart, and his grasp started to loosen a bit.

"I fell in love with you the moment I first saw you," he said with his face still half buried in my t-shirt. Now it was my heart that started to pick up in pace. "I know that sounds stupid ..." he continued, his voice raspy and broken, "...but it's the truth. And it wasn't a matter of pure physical attraction; I just saw you, and something clicked; and I knew the only thing I need to do in my life is to protect you." He placed his hands on my hips and pulled me away from him and stood up. He was taller than I, so he cupped my face in his hands and tipped my head up toward him.

"The only thing I care about is your safety," he said without even blinking. I grabbed his wrists gently and removed his hands from my face.

The silence had loosened the knot that had earlier tied up my throat; I was now confident enough to talk.

"Is that why you left me alone with Paul? Because it was safe?" I bit back and stepped around him, climbing into my bed.

"I never left," he said. "I had to make a choice that day whether to let you in on the whole situation or let you have coffee with Paul. I honestly felt you were safer not knowing, for the time being at least. I was there the whole time; you never left my sight. If anything would have happened, I would've been there in two seconds to pull you out of it."

fly

My back was turned to him, and I didn't respond. I couldn't. I didn't have anything to say. If the situation were reversed, I'd probably do the same thing, but I couldn't admit that to Kellen. The room was silent for a minute. My heart sank further than I thought possible when I thought he might have left. I was tired, and he might be mere feet away. My body was screaming, a full blown fire rumbling through my nervous system, begging to be held. Begging to feel the comfort and safety I felt when he was near me.

"Millie?" he said softly. Everything in me broke at the sound of his voice, the reassurance that he was still there. A tear escaped the corner of my eye and rolled over the bridge of my nose. My throat, once more, felt as though I'd swallowed an entire piece of bread without chewing it, so I murmured a "hmm," the best response I could muster.

Come lie with me; please come lie with me, I begged him in my mind, unable to set my pride and independence aside to ask out loud. My entire body felt as though it were about to burst; I was about to break into tears. I hadn't been aware it was possible to physically need someone so badly that I felt it in more than just my heart. A thought suddenly crossed my mind. If I needed him this badly now, when he's here, while he's alive, what'll happen when … when he's not here at all? I tried to take a breath in to ward off a flood of tears I could feel building up inside of me, but my lungs cut me off, and I burst into a hard sob.

He was next to me before I could even think about how to contain myself, rubbing my back and saying soothing words I couldn't even make out over my sobs. My body began to tremble as I cried from the moment he touched me, and I rolled toward him, as though I had absolutely no control, grasping at his shirt so I could get as close to him as humanly possible.

The moment I was pressed up against him, the sobbing subsided, and the sound of my breath still attempting to regain regularity was the only sound in the room. He had one arm wrapped around my head holding it to his chest, and the other was wrapped around my midsection holding me tight against him. My arm was caught between us, so I ran my fingers across his chest until I reached his port and then I stopped. There were no thoughts running through my head, no emotions surging through my body; everything was blank and calm, and I completely forgot that the world existed. A wave of relaxation washed over me; he had managed to snuff out the wildfire that had become my nerves.

"I need you," I told him, my voice muddled with tears.

This wasn't a thought or a ploy or fear. This felt like a fact of life. I would not survive this world without Kellen Anders. Two months ago I wasn't even aware he existed, but now? I couldn't conceive of life without him in it.

He kissed my forehead and swallowed hard. "You can sleep; I'll be right here," he whispered, but my eyes were already closed, and my breathing had already resolved itself into a steady rhythm.

I heard the roar of the crowd before I even opened my eyes. I had fallen asleep hard and fast pressed up against the warmth and comfort of Kellen, but my mind wasted no time at all before throwing me straight into a dream. I was lying on my side in the grass facing towards the bleachers. I sat up and wiped the grass and dirt from my face, trying to figure out my surroundings. It was dark out, and there was a soccer game going on. I quickly looked behind me for Corbin and his group, but no one was there. Maybe now that I knew what they were discussing there no longer was a need to investigate them. The crowd erupted, and I heard the announcer yell a drawn out "Goooooooaaaaaallll!" as I rose to my feet. I brushed off my pants and started walking towards the field. Something looked different, but I couldn't yet place what it was. I was standing at the corner of the bleachers looking out at the full field. The other team was jumping around in a small huddle on one side,, and Paul lay on his back on the ground on the other side. Kellen walked over to him and held out a hand to help him up. Paul looked at him for a short moment before accepting and then slowly pulled himself to his feet. Kellen patted him on the back and said something I was obviously too far away to hear, and they started to walk towards the other team. The other team, who was wearing blue jerseys. That was the thing that was out of place: in last week's game the other team was wearing green.

fly

This wasn't a memory; I had only been to one of the games, and this one wasn't it.

I frantically scanned my surroundings, taking note of certain things that might have been out of place or might have stuck out.

A horn blared, startling me, and the announcement of halftime came loudly through the speakers. I quizzically turned my head towards the announcer box, but I immediately dismissed it. Kellen was walking off of field with his team, and I noticed a row of men in suits standing on the sidelines talking to the coach. I inched closer to see what they were talking about and was almost knocked over by a player from the opposing team.

"Whoa," he said as he cupped his arm around my back to keep me from falling over. His hair was jet black and cut into a Mohawk. He reminded me of Rufio from the movie Hook.

"Sorry," I muttered staring into his huge dark eyes. He pulled me up straight and stepped around me to continue on towards wherever he's going. By the time the whole ordeal was over, the entire field and the bleachers were empty. Silence now filled the stadium, and I was standing alone.

I glanced up to the announcer box, but saw no one. Maybe I hadn't been imagining things before. Maybe it was Derek who I heard. I started up the steps toward the box.

When I opened the door, he was leaning back in his chair, hands hooked behind his head. He smiled widely at me, and I took a seat across from him. I looked out at the field, making sure it was still empty. "What was that?" I asked.

"A soccer game," he replied. I gave him a look, and he shrugged.

"I've never been to that game," I told him.

"No one has," he replied. We sat in silence for a moment while I gathered my thoughts.

"Paul's in trouble," I told him. He nodded.

"But he's not the one I have to save." The words escaped my mouth before I could give them any thought.

"Oh?" Derek's eyebrows raised.

"I don't know why I said that," I confessed.

"What do you feel when you're with him?" he asked.

"Sympathy, sadness, but never any fear or urgency." I was staring at a spot on the floor while searching my mind to get hold of my thoughts. I had no idea where the words were coming from.

"Amelia," he said to get my attention.

"Yeah?" I responded without looking up from the spot on the floor.

"You're thinking about it too much. You need to feel it. Most of the time it doesn't even require thought. Trust yourself," he urged.

"How do you trust someone who has already failed you?" I asked. I asked it because it was the truth. I had failed once before.

Once before, I had shown poor judgment. I had been blind to harsh realities. Someone had paid for that. Derek had paid for that.

"I'm not going to give you the speech about how my death wasn't your fault. I've said it all before, and repeating it is not going to change your mind. Amelia," eh took my hand in his, "I made a bad decision; it was my fault. If you're not going to trust yourself, you need to trust him." He pointed a finger toward the windows to my left. I glanced out, but no one was there.

I nodded. "God."

Derek let out a deep chuckle and shook his head. "Stand up," he instructed, and I did. I glanced out of the window again and saw someone sitting on the bottom row of the bleachers. Someone with bright-red, spikey hair wearing a soccer jersey. I looked over at Derek, and he shooed me out of his box.

I started down the bleachers, half expecting Kellen to disappear out of spite. I felt like I was constantly on the edge of discovery, never actually getting the entire story. I stepped quietly, afraid it wasn't real.

He sat on the very bottom of the bleachers, his head buried in his hands. I stood in front of him for a minute, wondering if I'd even be able to interact with him. I sometimes went unnoticed by people when I was dreaming; other times my physical connection to other people nearly knocked me on my ass.

I crouched to his level and rested a hand on his forearm, rubbing it lightly. He didn't respond.

"Hi baby," I said softly. He froze, but waited for a second before moving his hands from his face. He stared at me with a confused look. I was still standing in front of him, so I was taller than him and took advantage of that. I cupped his face in my hands as he had done to me so many times before and softly kissed him. I felt his body relax, and he brought his hands up and rested them on the backside of my knees. I pretended not to notice until they slowly started to creep upwards. When he reached the bottom of my butt I pulled away from him, his face still in my hands.

"What are you doing?" I asked playfully, brows raised.

He smirked. "Just testing my limits. This is my dream, after all," he said.

I shook my head. "No, it's not."

I looked up to the announcer box and saw Derek looking back down at us through the glass. I pointed. "This is my dream, I was just talking to Derek." Kellen turned to follow my gaze and saluted him. Derek saluted back. At first I thought this is just some weird boy thing, but then I saw the smirk on Kellen's face as he tapped the back sides of my legs. I began to ask questions at a rapid pace, but he quickly stood and kissed me, wrapping his arms around me as a protective barrier. My ability to think vanished quickly, taking the questions with it.

"I'm sorry," he said, his mouth an inch from mine, his words pouring straight into my mouth from his. "Were you saying something?"

"I… uh… hmm?" I breathed back into his mouth, bringing my lips back to his. He was still holding on to me, tipping me backwards just enough to give him complete control, determining whether I stayed standing or fell flat on my ass.

"Do you trust me?" he asked, slightly swaying me from side to side as if to enforce the fact that he had the power to drop me to the ground if he wanted to. I glanced up at the announcer box and once more saw Derek looking down at us. I closed my eyes and concentrated on what I felt.

I felt … like there was nowhere else in the world I should be. I felt sad for anyone else in the world who didn't even realize this kind of love existed. With my eyes still closed and my body in a near comatose trance, I nodded. I was suspended in the air, but I had never felt so protected and calm in my entire life.

"I've got this covered, Millie," he whispered in my ear and then kissed me once on the cheek. "I will take care of you." He pulled me back up, and I pressed my huddled body against him.

"Sweetheart," he said softly. "I have to go home. It's late."

When I opened my eyes, I was lying on my bed, and he was hovering over me with his jacket on, about to kiss my forehead.

"Kellen?"

"Sweetheart," he said, but I cut him off and finished his sentence for him.

"I have to go home. It's late," I said, as a twang of disappointment crept into my chest.

He paused and brought his face to the side of mine. "Hi baby," he whispered in my ear. "I'll see you tomorrow." He tucked the covers around the form of my body and left. I wanted to marvel over the fact that I was just there, with him, inside my – our – dream and considered he knew Derek, but I was incapable of doing anything other than immediately passing out.

chapter fourteen

Getting ready for school the next morning wasn't all that much fun. I had washed my hair, then conditioned it, and then conditioned it again because my mind was far too deep in thought about how I had somehow been *in* my head with Kellen.

And he *remembered* it.

And we had moments just like we would any other day.

By the time I got to school my thoughts had shifted entirely to think about everything I had learned the previous night about Paul and his drug problem and the fact that Adam was plotting revenge.

I sat in my parked car staring at the steering wheel a few moments before getting out of the car.

I had to do something.

I had to …

"Think Amelia, think!" I muttered out loud. I pressed my fingertips against my temples in frustration, willing the next best idea in saving lives to just magically appear, but to no avail. I was stuck with half of a brain.

The other half belonged to thoughts of Kellen.

"Alright Amelia," I said to myself as I gathered my books from my front seat, "give yourself one day without flooding your brain with Kellen." I grabbed hold of the car door handle and pulled myself out of the car. "I can do this," I said under my breath as I headed towards the school.

As always, I was early and unlike every other day, Kellen was nowhere to be found. I glanced around nervously for Adam and instead my eyes found Paul. I jumped up and started to head toward him right as Kellen stepped in front of me.

"Millie," he said sweetly.

"Kellen!" I was unable to withhold my surprise. "I have to go."

His face twisted in painful confusion.

"I was about to go talk to … Never mind, I just have to go, alright?" I had decided mid-sentence including him on things I was doing that might be considered dangerous was not my best move right now. He'd want to protect me from danger and whatever, and I would most likely not even realize he was engaging in actions to protect me. It was how we seemed to work.

I moved to step around him, and he mirrored my move.

"We should talk." He glanced over his shoulder quickly to see who it was I had been on my way to see , but immediately brought his attention back to me.

"Talk?"

"Yeah, about last night."

"What about it?"

"I don't know, maybe about how we were there, you know, together. I don't know about you, but it isn't often that I meet up with people in my Guardian dreams and am able to have a conversation we both remember in the morning."

I stopped trying to get around him and looked up at him, eyes wide.

"That's what I thought," he said as he stepped back, loosening his spatial reins. I tried to dodge to the left of him again, now at least making eye contact with Paul, but I failed miserably. Kellen stepped closer to me, greatly lessening the amount of space I had to work with.

"Millie," he started and took another step towards me. I backed up, bumping into the lockers. I was trapped and fidgeting nervously, not wanting to become distracted by him. I looked around impatiently, knowing that the second my eyes locked on his, I'd lose all brain function. My fingers balled into a fist and then stretched out again, a nervous tick I had developed when I needed more space.

"Hey," he said softly, hooking his finger under my chin, tilting it upwards. "Can I talk to you for a second?"

I somehow continued to avoid looking him straight in the face.

"I…" I grabbed hold of his arm and pulled it away from me. My body screamed at me, and I had to move around nervously in place to calm it. *We want that; what are you doing?!* my body screamed.

"I have to go. We can talk later, I promise. I just have to take care of something," I told him as I managed to twist past him. I glanced back and he was still standing less than a body space away from the lockers, staring at them as though he hadn't yet noticed I was missing from the scene. His stance of defeat made me pause, but not lose focus. I turned back around and headed towards Paul, ready to grab him by the arm and march him straight out of the school and into safety if I needed to.

"Amelia!" I heard Kellen call after me. His voice was pleading and scared, but I didn't turn around.

"Amelia Thompson … I love you."

I stopped dead in my tracks.

Paul was standing with his back against his locker looking around nervously. Kellen was behind me.

I wanted to turn around and tell him that I loved him back. I so desperately wanted him to know.

I stood frozen in time. What was that TV show called from the nineties? This girl did something like clap her hands or snap her fingers and everyone froze in time. *Out of This World?*

That's what it felt like. A second turned into a frozen minute.

I imagined turning back around and taking the few steps necessary to invade Kellen's space to tell him that I loved him more than I thought it was possible. In the end my brain won out, telling me I needed to keep myself on the side of good in order to even be able to enjoy Kellen's company in a few weeks.

I stepped forward, not able to glance back at him.

He'd forgive me ... right?

I could feel a gravitational pull weighing me down as I stepped further away from Kellen and closer towards Paul. My heart physically began to ache for me to turn back around. I turned back for one pleading second and saw Kellen leaning against the lockers staring up at the ceiling.

What have I done? What have I done? What have I done?

"Paul," I said gently as I reached out to lightly touch his arm. He jumped, and his books went flying in all directions.

"What the fuck, Amelia?!" His eyes were wild with fear.

"I'm sorry. I didn't mean to startle you!" I crouched down to grab a few pages that had attempted to escape.

"Oh God, I'm *so* sorry, Amelia. I didn't mean to yell." He pressed his palm against his forehead and squeezed his eyes shut as he stood back up. "I haven't slept, and I was thinking about … things, and I was watching for someone, and you're too damn quiet. You scared the crap out of me." He looked down at me and I could see his eyes were drained of life.

"Paul, you look like hell. Why don't you just go home and get some sleep?" I urged him.

It was a longshot and he didn't bite.

The bell rang.

"I have a test in Human Anatomy, and you can't make up a verbal test." He glanced back at me as he started to walk away. "Thanks for the concern, though. See you in math class, Amelia."

"Awesome," I muttered to myself as I started to head towards my first class. How many things could I screw up before nine a.m.?

chapter fifteen

The time leading up to lunch was treacherous. Remember when your boyfriend told you he loved you for the first time when you were walking away from him, trying to save a life? I wasn't sure whether to be angry with him or feel horrible he would say something so important and then watch me walk away from him.

He might have been really trying to keep me from going towards Paul, knowing what danger it held. He might have been in the moment and not cared about anything else. I might have broken his heart.

My leg bounced under my desk for the last five minutes of class until the bell rang dismissing us for our next period, mine being sociology with Kellen and Anthony. When I saw Kellen, was I supposed to acknowledge what had happened this morning or just let it go and pretend as though it never did?

This was the absolute worst timing ever. I needed to focus, but I couldn't imagine even a second of my life without knowing Kellen was going to be right by my side. That panicked thought made me rush to class faster than usual.

Usually when I arrived at class, Kellen was already there, but today my rush to get to him caused us to unexpectedly run into each other in the hallway. After a near-attempt at entering the room at the same time, he stepped back and held his hand out as to say 'after you,' and I quickly went to my seat. He walked past me seconds later, and a waft of his cologne drifted through the air following him, a wash of calm following suit.

I started to turn to talk to him since the bell letting us know class was starting hadn't even rung yet; but the second I moved, he suddenly jumped out of his seat and quickly walked up to the teacher. He nervously glanced back at me before hurriedly telling the teacher something and exiting the room without grabbing his books from his desk. I quickly turned back towards Anthony for an answer. He gave me a shrug and continued to take notes in his notebook.

Overachiever. Class hadn't even started. I glanced down at Kellen's books which were stacked neatly on his desk.

When I turned back around, I heard Anthony's phone vibrate against the chair from his pocket. I whipped back around to find him staring up at me, wide-eyed.

"Well?" I asked.

"Well, what?"

"That could be Kellen. Could you please check it?" I asked as though it was obvious.

He leaned forward. "The bell will ring the second I take it out of my pocket. Then it'll be taken away …" He paused. "…And we'll never know if it was Kellen or not."

He stared back at me, watching me closely to see if there was any sign he had won the argument.

I buckled after a few seconds of consideration.

"Fine," I replied. "But for the record, you could've been checking it while you were wasting time saying that." I turned back around to face forward.

I didn't hear a single thing the teacher said during the entire class period. I sometimes literally watched the seconds tick by on the clock, trying my hardest not to glance back at Anthony as if to say, *What are you waiting for?*

When the teacher stopped lecturing, Anthony finally snuck up to the front and asked to be excused for a bathroom break.

I waited very impatiently for him to come back, holding on to the top corner of my desk as though it were going to lift off. Eventually the kid to the right of me tapped my arm with his pen and asked if I was feeling okay. I tried to focus on the clock but that only made things go slower. I tried to focus on my breathing, but that just caused me to think I wasn't able to breathe properly which felt like the beginning of a panic attack, so I stopped that, too.

Eventually Anthony came back through the door and slipped a folded piece of paper onto my desk. I quickly unfolded it, unable to care what the teacher would think, had she been watching me. Anthony's tiny block writing took up a few lines on the page.

He's fine. He just forgot about something he had to take care of. He said to tell you he'd see you at lunch and not to worry. I'm supposed to also draw a heart, but I felt awkward doing that. Plus, you'd ask "Why is there a butt at the end of this sentence?"

I couldn't prevent a smile, and without turning around to glance at Anthony, I nodded my head a bit. I knew t he'd be watching patiently for my response, most likely because he was betting I would be upset by the note.

I didn't entirely trust that Kellen had left for a reason that wasn't worth worrying over. I wanted to tell him he was ridiculous for telling me he loved me in the middle of the school hallway. I wanted to throw my arms around him and kiss him softly and – more importantly – let him know how entirely needed he was. I needed him. *He needed to know I needed him.*

I felt like I couldn't breathe.

fly

The bell rang, and I jumped. I turned towards Kellen's seat out of habit just in time to see Anthony grabbing Kellen's stuff from his desk.

"See you at lunch Amelia," he said as he scurried past me.

My stomach dropped an inch.

I didn't feel good about this and I had no idea why.

2ff

chapter sixteen

I walked into the lunch room slowly. So slowly that I could easily have been mistaken for walking backwards or standing still. There were two reasons for this: I wasn't sure if Kellen would be there since he had been missing during sociology, nor did I know how I should act if he *was* at lunch because I hadn't had a chance to talk to him at all.

My eyes were focused on trying to follow the swarm of people in front of me, so of course I jumped a mile when I felt someone standing eerily close behind me. As always, I could tell it was him by the smell of his cologne. He nuzzled his face into my neck and slipped his arms around my waist pulling me closer to him.

"Come and eat lunch with me, Millie," he said softly with his face lost in my hair, lips almost touching my ear. He kissed the side of my head and headed towards the lunch line. Every inch of my body relaxed as I watched him walk away from me. *He's gorgeous,* I thought to myself for the thousandth time. *He's gorgeous, and I don't deserve him, and someday he'll realize that, too.*

"I love you, Kellen," I said quietly. I wanted to tell him that I did. I wanted him to feel as needed and important as I did but in the minutes between class and lunch, I had decided that no matter what, I needed to do what was best for him and that was *not* to keep him from what he deserved. He deserved more than me, of that I was sure.

By the time I got to the lunch line, there were few people around. I stood alone at the end of the line, tray in hand, taking a moment to watch Kellen and Anthony talking to Scott and Matt at the table. I loved my life, but I didn't feel like I deserved it. I walked over to the table and set my tray down just in time to become an unwilling participant in the conversation.

"Amelia, this is really important," Matt said as I sat down.

"Okay?" I responded but my eyes were watching Kellen as he scribbled something down on paper and worriedly looked over his shoulder.

"Amelia!" Matt said over my thoughts.

"I'm sorry, what?" I turned back towards him and focused on whatever it was that he was asking me.

"Leonard Cohen. "Hallelujah." Happy song or sad song?" he asked.

"Hallelujah?" I couldn't seem to recall the song on the spot. Kellen quietly got up from his seat and kissed me on the forehead as he walked by.

"We're not friends anymore," Anthony said as he threw his apple core into his empty lunch bag.

"What?" I said muffled through a bite of a hot ham sandwich.

"Amelia, seriously? You know the song." He looked at me as if he was in agony and then started to sing. It wasn't shocking to me that he sounded like he had sung the song before. Matt chimed in and became overly dramatic with his hand gestures and finished the line with his hand outstretched towards me. My head picked up where Matt left off, and I closed my eyes remembering the way the music flows with the words of the song, just as I'm sure Cohen had intended it to.

I opened my eyes to see both Matt and Anthony looking at me intently waiting for my answer. "It takes away emptiness when I'm sad and it gives me confidence when I'm happy. It's both," I answered without thinking. An eruption of disagreement and arguments forced my eyes down to my untouched food, and I noticed a piece of paper was tucked under the corner of my tray. I grabbed for it and as I was about to open it, until someone behind me knocked over a chair and the entire cafeteria broke out in a chorus of "Heyyyyy!!"

fly

I winced. Overpowering sounds made my brain go into a frenzy.

I rolled my eyes and turned back to the table. On the piece of paper were three simple words scribbled into the center of the paper: *I love you.*

Anthony started to sing again as Matt and Scott started a different argument.

The lunch room was still unnecessarily loud from the excitement that surged through the crowd when the chair tipped over. I was so deep in thought that I didn't immediately notice when the entire room went silent and the only sound was a single spoon bouncing to a rest on the tile floor.

The next minute seemed to go in slow motion. I looked up at Anthony and Matt who seemed to still be arguing and then over to where the spoon had fallen. It didn't take me long to pinpoint the location since an entire tray of food falling to the floor followed it and continued to be the only sound I could hear. I followed the spoon and the tray and then up a few pairs of legs to see Adam standing only a foot away from Paul. The room remained silent in my mind, the rest of the world entirely unaware of what was going on, until the sound of Adam loading a clip into his gun rang through my ears. He held it directly to Paul's face. All it took was for someone to scream "Gun!" and everyone started to scatter.

184

I stood at my seat, glancing away for a second from Adam and Paul when a crowd of people started to rush by me. Anthony was holding out his hand saying my name, but I could only read it off his lips. Everything in the room was muted, and in my mind the guitar stroke of "Hallelujah" played in a slow rhythm. I simply blinked at him and turned back toward Adam and Paul just in time to see the boy with bright-red, spiked hair step between them.

Kellen.

Kellen, no.

The sound of the world came crashing back to my eardrums like a tidal wave. It was the sound of my own voice screaming Kellen's name that had broken the silence in my mind.

"Paul, get out of here," Kellen instructed.

"Paul, if you fucking move, I'll shoot you," Adam warned. "Stay right the fuck where you are. Kellen, move. Now."

Kellen didn't budge except to make sure that he was between Paul and Adam at all times.

In the moment I realized nothing else mattered; I also realized I might never have the chance at it again. I felt an arm wrap around my midsection pulling me backwards as I lunged forward. I wriggled in a fit of rage and panic as Anthony pulled me towards the hallway.

"Anthony!" I thrashed my legs which were not currently touching the ground. "Kellen!" The heel of my shoe connected hard with Anthony's shin, and he yelped. He loosened his grip just enough for me to free myself from his arms. I took a few stumbling steps forward before I tripped.

I wanted to get up, to keep moving towards Kellen, but the only thing I could feel was a constriction of every single part of my body into a solid state at the same time my whole body was completely falling apart. My muscles literally would not let me bring myself to my feet.

The song, it could be both angry and hopeful at the same time. All it took was a twist of a note or the pitch of a word, and it all changed in an instant. I looked up where Kellen stood between Paul and Adam. They were all yelling: Adam at Paul, Kellen at Adam, Paul pleading with the both of them. Adam raised his arm at a forty-five degree angle and fired a shot. The plastic guard on a light fixture shattered to pieces and fell to the ground in a heaping mess mixed with glass from the bulb. I threw my arms over my head as a reflex.

"Adam, think about this. How much money does he owe you? I'll pay it." Kellen's voice was oddly calm as he tried to reason with someone who had a gun only inches from his face.

"I don't want your *fucking* money, *Kellen*!" I could see spit flying from Adam's mouth as he spoke.

"Why? We'll settle up, and this can be over," Kellen said.

"This isn't about the money any more. This is about the fact that this piss ant, this privileged mother-fuck, thinks he can fuck me over. Get the *fuck* out of the way, you dumb shit," Adam yelled as he shook the gun in Kellen's face.

"No," Kellen responded sternly.

Adam brought the gun to Kellen's forehead and glanced over in my direction. "Do you want me to blow your brains out in front of Amelia?"

My heart, already pounding hard in my chest, stopped beating at the sound of my name. I couldn't swallow. I couldn't think. The room grew silent. Silent enough to hear the quiet sound of someone approaching in the hallway.

"Drop the weapon," a loud voice boomed. I looked past where Kellen was standing to see police officers with guns pointed at Adam.

I quickly looked to the hallway to my left and right only to see the same scene. How in the hell did they get here so fast?

"Put the weapon on the ground and raise your hands in the air where we can see them," they warned for the second time.

Adam narrowed his gaze on Kellen and shifted the direction of his gun slightly to the right of Kellen's head. It was now pointed straight at Paul. If Adam had one chance to shoot, he wasn't going to waste it on Kellen. I watched him think for a second, most likely only to put the fear of God into Paul, but the moment that Adam heard more officers pull their weapons to point at him, he lowered the gun and slowly put it on the ground. His arms rose above his head, and a group of men dressed in black protective gear rushed toward the three of them.

My knees gave way, and I fell to the ground. My breaths had become long, drawn-out sobs in which I was choking on the very air I was supposed to be breathing. A police officer was at my side trying to coax me into standing up and moving out of the way, but I was shaking so hard I wasn't sure whether I'd be able to stand. I looked up and saw they had Kellen sitting on a chair surrounded by police officers trying to take down his information. His elbows were on his knees, and he was running his hands viciously through his spiked hair turning it into a red puff.

He glanced over at me, and when he saw my distress, he mouthed the words, "It's okay," before answering whoever had asked him a question last.

I tried to take one more gasp of air, but my lungs completely refused to cooperate. In that moment the world went quiet and black.

chapter seventeen

I awoke to the sound of a steady beep coming from somewhere above me. I was afraid to open my eyes, afraid to move. I wasn't entirely sure where I was, and the last thing that I remembered happening was seeing a gun held to Kellen's face.

Kellen.

My eyes flew open, and I tried to sit up but my body didn't follow the instruction. Instead I waited for my eyesight to gain focus and hurriedly glanced around. I found the source of the beeping, a small machine to the left of me that was flashing red and green numbers. I couldn't read them. I looked down to my right where I found a sleeping Kellen, half in a chair, half rested on my bed. When I went to lift my arm to touch him, I noticed there were tubes attached to a slab of tape on the top of my hand. I followed the tube with my eyes up to a bag of clear fluid that was hanging over my head.

I wasn't entirely sure what was going on. The room was silent except for the beeping of the machine. I slowly lifted my hand and ran my fingers through the soft tuft of Kellen's bright-red hair.

He didn't wake, but he still leaned toward my touch.

"Kellen," I whispered, but he didn't budge. "Kellen," I then said in a normal voice.

"Millie," he responded groggily with his eyes still shut, and then a second later, he realized where he was and what my talking meant.

"Amelia!" he said, his eyes flying open as he fumbled to his feet. "How do you feel?"

"I feel fine, just a little sleepy ... and cold," I said.

"Do you want me to get you a blanket?" he asked.

I nodded, and he started to walk towards the door. "Wait," I called out, a panic rising inside of me without reason. I glanced over at the blinking numbers on the machine; they were jumping around.

"Or you could lie with me?" I shifted over toward the left side of my bed hoping he would join me. My eyes started to grow heavy, and I just wanted to go back to sleep. He hesitated at the door for a few seconds and then stepped backwards towards my bed. He eyed the tubes that ran from my IV to my arm and the pulse monitor that was clamped on my finger. I held my arms off the side of my bed to show him he wouldn't be interfering with any of my wires, and he carefully slipped into the bed. I propped myself up on my elbow to give him space to slide his arm under me, and he did so without a second's pause.

Once my head was on his chest, I felt calmer. I sat there in silence for a moment just listening to the thump, thump of his heart. He reached over for something on the side of my bed, but I couldn't see exactly what it was.

"How can I help you?" a voice boomed into the speaker built in to the side of my bed. I hurriedly glanced up at Kellen with a confused look on my face.

"She's awake," he responded.

"Okay, we'll be in shortly, thank you."

The nurse button. He had grabbed for the nurse button. So much for a few moments of peace.

"Kellen," I mumbled, my voice full of sleep. "What happened?"

"You don't remember?" he asked. "You passed out in the cafeteria."

"I figured that much. I meant …" I searched my mind for words, but I couldn't think of the right ones. If I didn't word the question properly, he could easily get away with not answering it with the information I was looking for. "I meant … did you know that Adam had a gun?"

His breath poured over the top of my head as he heavily exhaled. Of course, with perfect timing, the nurse came through the door, and Kellen quickly got off of my bed.

"Amelia! Nice to see you awake. How are you feeling?" she asked as she grabbed hold of my IV bag and started to make notes on a pile of pages attached to a clipboard.

"Fine," I said quickly.

"Any headache or nausea?" she asked as she applied a blood pressure cuff to my arm. She finally looked at me instead of the equipment and smiled sweetly. I shook my head.

"Do you remember what happened?" she asked, her eyes now fixed firmly on me.

"I fainted," I answered. She continued to stare as though she expected more. "There was a student with a gun in the cafeteria, and it was pointed at my boyfriend and then I fainted." I realized quickly she wasn't sure if I had remembered the 'before fainting' part.

She nodded and started to fiddle with the machines again. "You didn't so much faint as you passed out. People who faint usually become responsive fairly quickly after." She looked back over at me. "You were out for a few hours." Just then the doctor strolled in with a huge smile on his face. I had never met anyone else in my life who can make a mustache actually look like it's a symbol of joy.

"Amelia!" he bellowed in a sing-song voice. "Stick out your tongue."

"What?" I asked, confused.

"Millie, it's like this," Kellen piped up and let his tongue hang out of his mouth.

"Precisely!" the doctor praised him.

My face was still crinkled in confusion, but I followed suit. He stepped closely, and looked down at it.

"Beautiful!" he exclaimed, as though I had done something well. He walked his fingers up and down my neck feeling for... what is it exactly that doctors are feeling for when they do that kind of thing? He grabbed a pen and shined a light in each eye. "How are you feeling?" he asked.

"I'm fine. I'm just a bit sleepy," I answered.

"Well, you're looking great, and you're no longer dehydrated." He grabbed my IV bag and said something to the nurse that I couldn't quite understand. "We're just waiting on some test results and then you'll be good to go! How's that for ya, kiddo?"

I nodded in response.

"Great." He smiled back at me again, and I swear his mustache smiled, too. "Just let me know if anything else comes up in the meantime, okay?" He gave a small raise of the hand to Kellen and sang "Adios!" on his way out of the door.

The nurse stuck a needle into a branch of my IV line and smiled at me. "Just to help you rest," she said. She said nothing further and left the room. Kellen started toward my bed, and I could do nothing but give him a halfhearted confused look.

"The tongue becomes dry if you're dehydrated. It gets all pale and dry-looking. It's how they can tell if you're going to need more fluids or not," he told me. I nodded. I hadn't asked about it, but I was sure he knew I was wondering. I blinked, but it became harder to reopen my eyes. I felt Kellen lean in and kiss me on the forehead a few times.

"I'll call you later," he whispered. I wanted to protest. In my head, I was protesting. I wanted answers from him. I wanted to know what he knew about Adam and the gun, but I simply couldn't move. I was too tired. The drug the nurse had just given to me forced me back into sleep, and I welcomed the weight of it. The force of the sleep was nothing worth fighting against, especially when you're never able to obtain it on your own because your mind is racing at a million miles per minute.

I heard the door click closed followed by complete silence and then the drug took over, and I let it consume me and bring with it dark, silent oblivion.

chapter eighteen

On the ride home from the hospital, my grandma informed me she had received a phone call from the school stating they were not going to have classes the following day because too many parents were concerned about sending their children back to the school after today's incident.

My phone buzzed in my pocket as I was getting out of the car to go into the house.

Are you busy tomorrow? Kellen had asked.

Now that I hear we don't have school I'm not, I replied.

Good... can I have you for the day then?

The whole day? What do you want to do? I'm not sure I can do much because I was in the hospital today.

I've already cleared it with Granmillie, no worries. I promise not to take you for a cross- country run or anything.

You asked my grandma?

fly

Yeah, at the hospital ... I just wanted to make sure it was alright to hang out with me for the day before you got all excited.

You assumed I'd say yes?

Millie... have you SEEN me? Who wouldn't??

Kellen even had a way of making vanity cute. Why wouldn't he?

I suddenly remembered the events leading up to the lunch-time event, and my stomach flipped. I forgot about how he had told me that he loved me and how I had so rudely acted like it didn't matter.

It did.

I swore to myself in those moments that the gun was pointed at Kellen's head I wouldn't let life continue without his knowing how I felt. I had to keep that promise.

I roamed around my house for a few minutes trying to convince myself that since I had been sleeping all day, the extreme fatigue I felt was something I could chalk up to oversleeping, but I eventually gave in and headed down to my room.

I fell asleep while lying on my bed debating whether or not I wanted to take a shower. After dreamless sleep all day, I was actually happy to open my eyes and see Derek sitting across from me in the announcer booth above the soccer field.

"Rough day Amelia?" he asked softly as he held out a hand to help me up. For some odd reason I was sitting curled in a ball underneath the counter. I looked up at him and nodded.

196

"I think I'd rather stay down here if you don't mind. It feels kind of safe right now," I said as I glanced at his outstretched hand. I was surprised by my own words.

"Derek … what happened today? How did it happen?" I was asking him the questions he should have been asking me. I knew he had the answers, and I knew he wasn't going to give them to me. I had to ask anyway.

"I'm working against Adam," I said to him.

He still only stared down at me.

"Is Kellen working against Adam, too? We're working towards the same thing, right?" My voice was beginning to become panicked and demanding.

"Maybe you should talk to Kellen about this. You're seeing him tomorrow, right?" he asked, his voice still calm and quiet.

Unexpectedly, I started to cry.

Derek got up from his chair and joined me under the counter. His knees stuck up awkwardly since he was far taller than I was and didn't fit very well in my confined space.

"Just talk to Kellen tomorrow," he said once again. "And maybe you should try to see Adam, too."

"What?!" I glared over at him.

"He's sitting in jail right now. No one is going to bail him out; that I can promise you. You'll be safe; there will be a glass partition between you. When you wake up, call the jail and set up a visit with him."

fly

When I glanced up at Derek, he was looking at me very intently. I could tell in the way he was telling me to see Adam that he wasn't supposed to be telling me these things at all, so I didn't ask him any more questions.

"Amelia?" he asked as we sat side by side scrunched up under the counter. We had both been staring at the wall across from us for some time now.

"Yeah Derek," I said, my voice coming out hoarse and phlegmy.

"I know I've told you before, but you really have to listen."

I nodded and looked over at him.

"Not just literally, but with your heart and body. Whatever you feel is most likely right, so you need to listen to yourself."

I flashed back to the party that had ultimately led to Derek's death. I had been walking toward him as he played beer pong on a ping pong table, and Rob had stopped me.

"Hey Amelia. Come with me; I have to talk to you," Rob had said with a huge smile on his face. When I looked up at him, the room became muted, and all I could hear was the bouncing of the ping pong ball on the table. I looked back at Rob, and he was saying something else, but I couldn't make out the words.

The ball clipped a cup and bounced backwards. I heard it, but I didn't look back because right then Rob grabbed my hand and started leading me away. The moment he touched me, the sound came back to the room, and my heart started to beat in a panic.

Every nerve in my body seemed to be screaming 'run,' but at the time I had chalked it up to nerves. When I glanced up, I was looking at Derek, and we were back in the announcer booth, now standing.

"See? You just have to listen," he said as he sat back on his chair and methodically swiveled side to side.

chapter nineteen
kellen

I was in her driveway at 8 a.m. I knew she wouldn't be awake yet, much less ready, but I couldn't stand one more moment of watching the minutes change on the clock on the stove. I needed to have her very close to me. I casually walked up to the front door and softly knocked. I knew her grandmother would be awake, and I was willing to bet she wouldn't be anything less than happy to see me here.

"Good morning Granmillie," I said as I flash her my best 'love me' smile.

"Why, Kellen! What a nice surprise! Come on in. I'm just making breakfast." She held the door open and I followed her to the kitchen. As I suspected, Amelia wasn't up yet.

"Amelia is still sleeping," she whispered as she scooped scrambled eggs onto a plate in front of me. "She did tell me the two of you had an outing planned for the day, though. Oh, I'm so glad, because after the horrible day the two of you had yesterday, you deserve a day away." She let her gaze fall a bit and seemed to be deep in thought.

I cleared my throat. "I'll take good care of her, Mrs. Jackson, I promise."

She turned toward me and smiled sweetly. "Oh, I know Kellen. It's just … that poor girl has been through so much in her lifetime. I'm really glad she has you. You're the good in her life." She walked back to the stove and set the pan of eggs down. She then took out a large kitchen knife and stabbed me right in the gut.

No, she didn't.

But that was what her words had felt like.

You're the good.

Just then I heard Amelia making her way up the stairs. She was groggy at first, and her hair was a mess, barely still in her ponytail. Her face was devoid of makeup, and she looked more beautiful than ever. I watched her eyes focus and then become wide when they landed on me. Her hands immediately went to fix her hair.

"Kellen!" she exclaimed. She tugged downward on her t-shirt and cleared her voice. She clicked on her phone, most likely to check the time.

fly

"I'm early," I said as I winked at her. "I was too eager to start our day." I smiled at her and it was genuine. She was so damn beautiful. I took out my phone and quickly texted her.

I wish I could scoop you up and take you back downstairs and curl up next to you in bed.

I watched her read the text and try her best not to smile, but her eyes melted. I was watching her too intently to miss that part.

"I'm, um, going to go shower," she said as she turned back toward the stairs.

"Amelia Rose! I made breakfast!" her grandmother proclaimed.

She paused for a moment and caught herself on the stair railing. She bit her bottom lip as she debated what to do.

I wanted to bite her lip, too. Not fair.

She glanced back at the table where her grandmother was already making her a plate, and she walked over with a pained expression on her face.

After she finished eating, she went downstairs to take a shower, and I played a game of cribbage with her grandmother who talked about this year's garden crop and the change of birds recently at her feeder. I smiled and nodded a lot, and all the while repeated in my head. *You're going to hate me one day.*

"Where are we going?" Amelia asked as she tied her shoes and reached back to adjust the height of her seat belt. I glanced over at her and smiled.

My smile was genuine. I wanted to stare at her and memorize every single dip and curve of her face. Every freckle, every loose curl. I wanted her to take up all of the previously used and unused space in my brain.

"The water fountain to start out. I eventually have to be somewhere later this morning but I was hoping you'd come with me?" I asked.

"Where?"

I smiled at her, but I knew it was a weak one. She looked out of the window, and I quickly slipped my hand into hers. I felt her flinch at first, but she tightened her grasp.

"Can we get coffee first? I didn't exactly have time this morning. Early visitor and all." She raised her eyebrows at me. I laughed in response. I pulled her hand toward my face and kissed it. We were stopped at a red light, so I looked over at her and smiled.

"Anything for you Millie," I answered, and I really did mean it.

After she got her coffee, we sat on a bench watching the fountain. She pulled her knees up to her chest, and I took the opportunity to pull her off balance and toward me. She stiffened at first, but then immediately relaxed against me.

I closed my eyes and breathed in her scent. Memorize, memorize, memorize. She smelled like girl soap and hairspray and perfume and everything good. I rested my forehead against the side of her head.

"I have something for you," I said softly with my face buried against her hair.

"Oh?" she asked.

"Yeah, hold out your hand," I told her. She did as I asked, and I slid a charm into her hand and quickly closed her fingers around it. She opened her hand and sat up. I didn't wait for her to ask about it.

"I thought you could wear it with the medal I gave you." I watched her for a moment as she stared at the silver wing in her hand.

"When you can no longer run nor walk nor crawl, fly," I tell her.

She unclasped the necklace I had previously given to her and slid the chain through the silver hoop on the wing. She didn't say a single word, but she took a sip of her coffee with her other hand grasped around the charms on the necklace.

"Kellen …" She looked me straight in the eyes. I wanted to live in her eyes. See the world the way she saw it. More than that, I wanted to show her herself the way that I saw her.

"Where do you have to go?" she asked.

I sighed and folded my hands into my lap. I stared at the water as it fell from spouts in the center of the fountain. I would tell her. But would I tell her the whole truth? Was it fair to do that?

Or did I spend the rest of my life with her blissfully unaware of what was to come?

"To the hospital," I said wearily.

She looked at me with concern.

I put my hand to my chest. "I have to get my port removed and have a few tests done," I told her. I could see her chest suddenly rising and falling more rapidly. She was processing it.

"I can take you home instead if you'd like?" I asked.

She shook her head in response and grabbed my hand.

I wanted to tell her the truth. But I was not a good enough person to do that.

chapter twenty

amelia

I had never been in the cancer wing of a hospital before. I guess I had never really given much thought about what it would even be like. I walked in hand-in-hand with Kellen, but as soon as I saw all eyes turn to us, I slinked behind him a bit. People were reading the paper, sipping coffee, watching the news on television, some crocheting even. No matter what they were doing, they paused when the doors slid open. They sullenly stared as if attempting to figure out which of the two of us was sick. I was sure my attempt to hide and Kellen's knowing exactly where to go let them know it was him. They turned back to their activities and then it was me who was quickly glancing at all of them and noticing wigs, bandanas, and proud bald heads. Their loved ones who sat next to them looked worn and tired

I looked back at Kellen and saw that the admission person was wrapping an admit bracelet around his wrist and methodically babbling some sort of check-in instruction to him. I wondered to myself if anyone had overheard why he was here. Were they jealous he would be able to get his port out? Did they wish they were Kellen? He tugged on my hand, and I looked up at him.

"This way, Millie," he said as he started down the hallway. Part of me was grateful I didn't have to sit in the waiting room with everyone else. I didn't want to squirm in my seat trying to avoid looking at everyone wondering what their stories were.

We walked into a small locker room, and he led me toward a chair in the small waiting area. He crouched in front of me with his eyes fixed on my necklace. He gently reached to straighten it out. I froze and swallowed hard, but in doing so, I realized my mouth had gone dry.

"Millie," he said as he looked into my eyes and cupped his hand to the side of my face. I wanted to respond, but I couldn't. My breathing was now deep and fast, and the more that I breathed him in at this distance, the more I forget how to act like a human being.

He smirked and kissed me once, but paused for quite a while before separating his lips from mine. I was breathing in his air, and it felt, unfairly, like better air than my lungs had ever previously experienced. He went to stand, but paused, touching our foreheads and noses together briefly. "Thank you for staying with

fly

me," he said quietly and then quickly kissed my forehead. He walked away toward a locker, pulled out a gown, and moved into the changing room.

I sat frozen for a minute. Loving Kellen felt a lot like what I imagine it would feel like to exist out in outer space.

It was quiet.

It was peaceful.

Everything was beauty, and nothing else really mattered.

You just simply were. The rest of the world felt so small and irrelevant.

Given my current mission and life thus far, this idea seemed very surreal. Was it possible for one person to do this to another? I was falling deeper in love with Kellen despite all of my attempts not to.

At that moment Kellen walked out of the changing room wearing nothing but a gown and some slipper socks. He turned to put his bag of clothes in a locker, but then quickly remembered two things: One, I was here to hold his bag of clothes and two, hospital gowns aren't notorious for covering backsides. My lower lip automatically tucked inward, and my eyes grew wide as he caught me looking his way when he quickly turned back toward me. Soccer players have *muscles*. I was staring straight ahead as he tied his gown shut in back and went to engage a fellow gown wearer to discuss the latest sports section of the paper. My mind was no longer in outer space.

Now my mind was in Kellen's space. I was slipping through that opening in his gown and around to the front side of his torso, imagining how warm his skin would be under my hands as they followed the rise and fall of all of those muscles. Kissing him would be so …

I was completely lost in thought when I registered that Kellen had said my name twice. My face flushed with embarrassment as if he were able to see where my thoughts had been. I quickly fumbled with my purse and his bag and got up to exit the room with him. I had never in my entire life had thoughts like that. The closest I can honestly say I had ever been that lost was when I was enamored with Rob, but it was nowhere near what I was feeling at that moment. Entirely different actually. Additionally, there was the fact it was a different scenario than the one with Rob because Rob was purposely trying to distract me from my mission. He probably had some ability to play with my emotions because of it.

We were directed to a curtained-off bed where the nurse checked a few of Kellen's vitals and told him that someone would be back to give him an IV and then soon after take him back for the procedure.

"Millie, come here," Kellen said as he moved to one side of the bed and patted the other side. I gave him a crooked smile, but the sullen look on his face couldn't be disputed. I climbed up beside him, and he pulled me up against him so my ear was at his chest. The sound of his heart beating made the world melt away. He began to grab curls from my hair and twist them around his finger.

"Will you be here when I come out?" he asked me. I frowned, but I was in too much of a trance to lift my head and show him the puzzled look on my face in response.

"Of course," I said with as much enthusiasm as I could manage. I seriously didn't understand how I could feel like I was literally melting into him. My body felt like lead, and I was suddenly now so very tired.

"Amelia," he whispered. He used my real name. I was so tired I couldn't comprehend what he was trying to tell me. I made some sort of grunting noise in response. I intended the sound to include words, but I was just so damned comfortable. I heard a nurse whisper to him that it would be alright, that he didn't need to make me move when she connected the IV.

It's a good thing she didn't, because in that moment I could no longer fight the heaviness I was feeling and I fell into a deep sleep.

chapter twenty one

I fell asleep.

To this day, I remember the peace and tranquility of it –
resting against Kellen. Funny how I'd been able to find such
serenity amongst the beeping and humming of hospital equipment.

I woke up in a dream. I was in a large waiting area of sorts.
It was hushed in the room despite the fact that all of the chairs
were occupied. The wall across from me was lined in artwork. I
couldn't quite make out what it said underneath each piece. I
turned in my chair but the only things behind me were big bay
windows looking out onto a parking lot. *Dodge County Jail Visitor
& Huber Parking,* a sign read.

I glanced back at my peers with new understanding and
then up at the artwork. Inmate artwork. A loud buzzer sounded,
and a set of double doors swung open to reveal a female guard.

Everyone got up and started toward her. They'd done this before; they knew the routine.

"Please remove all jewelry and empty your pockets into this bin. Remove your shoes and walk through the metal detector. Lockers are located behind you for your belongings. You will receive a coin for them when you've walked through. Sign in at the visitor's log and then wait by the elevator. When we are all ready, I will escort you up to the visitation area. Does anyone have any questions?"

She sounded methodical as she listed off instructions. She probably had said it all a million times. She was hardened, but she smiled and nodded at me as I walked through the metal detector. She handed me a coin, and I headed over to the lockers even though I didn't really have anything to drop off. The room grew louder now, everyone clearly excited to see whoever they were there to visit. We all shuffled into the elevator.

Yesterday's phone call to the jail led me to find out I would not be able to visit Adam unless he had me on an approved visitor list. Yes, I checked and no, he did not. When everyone was done, we all crammed into a pretty large elevator. People were now grinning and giddy with excitement. I had no idea what to expect. The closest thing I knew about jail visitation is what I had seen on television.

When we stepped out of the elevator, there was a distinct smell of antibacterial soap. I stepped aside so the crowd rushed past and I could follow suit. I watched as they went down a long hallway and one by one disappeared into little cubbies that were lined up on the right side of the hall. I glanced over as I walked by, and people were leaning over a counter with their faces close to the glass that separated them from the inmate. One girl and her assumed boyfriend were both sitting on the counters on either side of the glass to appear as though they were cuddled up together. No one was wasting any time jumping into conversation.

I walked past nine cubbies until I reached the only empty one. As I slowly passed by the last divider, I saw him shrugging down his dark blue jumpsuit, revealing a white t-shirt underneath as he tied the arms at his waist. His face lit up when he saw me, and I just stood there for a second staring in disgust.

"Amelia!" Adam said as he held out his arms. "Come, have a seat with me," he said as he motioned to my plastic chair. He rested his forearms on his side of the counter and eagerly smiled at me. Smug asshole. I swallowed hard and slid into the chair on the edge of it as though I might need to bolt at any second.

"I knew you'd find a way to see me," he said with a smile. His head was still resting in his hand. He looked as though he had won the lottery.

"Kind of hard to finish your job behind bars, Adam," I said.

He erupted in laughter. "You think I'm alone, Amelia?" He was resting back in his chair now, his fingers intertwined, smile still wide across his face. My mouth had gone dry.

"He wasn't caught," a voice said from behind me.

"Were you?" Kellen asked Adam as he stepped forward towards the glass. "He did exactly what he needed to do, set the plan into motion."

My head whipped up to look at Kellen.

"That means …" I started out.

"There are two missions," Kellen finished as he pushed away from the counter. Kellen quickly turned around and walked away, and I started to follow when Adam leaned towards the glass again and sing-songed my name.

"Hey Amelia," he said, his grin still wide. "They should have left you to die. You were never worth more than what your dad did to you anyway."

I stood up and my chair screeched as it moved backwards. My heart was pounding hard in my chest, but I tried to appear unaffected. When I was out of his sight, I ran towards the elevator. When the doors opened, Kellen was standing inside. He grabbed my arm and pulled me toward him holding my head against his chest. It was only then, with the sound of his heart echoing through my ear, that I was able to calm down.

I opened my eyes and blinked a few times, confused about where I was. Kellen was sleeping in a hospital bed next to whatever it was that I was lying on.

A nurse quietly stepped into the room, her expression sullen. "Did I wake you?" she asked.

I shook my head.

"Oh good," she whispered. "When he wakes up, he just has to stay here a half hour and as long as he's feeling fine, he can go home," she told me. She then stepped towards me and rested a hand on my shoulder. "I'm so sorry," she said and then slipped out of the room.

Sorry? Did she know what had happened at the school?

"Best post-surgery wake up ever," Kellen said hoarsely.

I flew over to his side. "Hey!" I said, smiling. "Last time I saw you, we were in an elevator," I said trying to distract him.

"Can you be here for all of my surgeries?" he asked pulling me closer.

"I could," I said, "but I believe that will be the last one."

"Can you stay with me?" he asked.

"Well, obviously, I told you I would drive you home. You can leave in a half hour as long as you're feeling okay."

He shook his head. "No, I meant when you take me to my house. Stay with me. Watch a movie. Let's be normal teenagers."

His plea for normality was one I couldn't turn down. "Okay," I told him. *Okay.*

chapter twenty two
kellen

"Millie? Why'd you do it?" I asked.

We were lying on the bed in the spare room at my house, parent's rules. There were no curtains in the room, so the moonlight was pouring through the three large windows against which the bed stood. Amelia was tucked up against my side, and we were reverting to childhood by making shadow puppets on the ceiling. Her puppet slowly ducked back into the shadows. She sighed because she knew what I was asking. Every Guardian had once died, at his own hand. It was our duty once we were granted a second chance to step into the Guardianship.

"I overdosed on pills. My brother found me when I fell and knocked a painting off of the wall in the basement. I coded on the way to the hospital," she answered methodically.

I rubbed her arm and pointed my puppet dog to look at her. "Why didn't you want to live anymore?" I asked. I felt her body stiffen at my side.

"I, umm ..." she trailed off and then began to cry. Not just soft cry, but big heavy sobs. Could my heart break from a sound? Because I think it did. Panic arose in me, and I wanted to do whatever needed to be done to undo her heartache. It was a stupid thing of me to ask her, but I couldn't prevent myself from wanting to know every little thing about her. I reached over and cradled her face in my hand. It felt like her face was made to fit my palm, as corny as that sounded. It really did fit perfectly. How did I ever exist before she came into my life? I wanted to devour her pain, take it away from her, make it my own. So I did the only thing I could think of doing: I kissed her. Softly at first, as though I could let her meld into me and absorb whatever it was that made her hurt like this. I felt her body start to relax, and she became putty at my side. I wanted to kiss her forever, but I also wanted to apologize profusely for making her sad.

"Millie," I muttered as I pulled away from her. Her eyes were still closed and her lips slightly parted.

"Millie, I'm so sorry. That was stupid of me," I whispered only an inch away from her mouth.

"Hmm?"

I couldn't help it; I started to laugh at her incoherence.

fly

"Amelia," I said as I tried to compose myself. "Are you with me?"

"When I kiss you," she said, "my mind goes completely blank. I can't think or feel fear or sadness. All I can do is kiss you and be aware of only you." Her eyes were still closed as she spoke. I pulled back and kissed her forehead.

"I think that means you love me," I teased.

"I think I wish you were the only other person who existed in this world," she responded.

"I'll take it," I said.

"I do, Kellen. I do love you." Her eyes were still closed and I could feel her body getting heavy.

"I know you do."

"Oh?"

"Yeah, you drew a heart in the sand in my Zen sand box," I reminded her. She didn't respond. "I'm supposed to take you home in a half hour," I whispered but I know she didn't hear me because she had fallen asleep still clinging to me. I should have slept, too, but I wouldn't. Not yet. I wanted to be here in this moment with her. I wanted to memorize how she felt against my body. I wanted to take this moment and live in it.

Live.

My hand absentmindedly went to where my port had previously been in my chest. The port I just had removed. The port that I will no longer need.

fly

I wanted all of my days to be with her.

"Shit," I said under my breath as I awoke sitting across from Derek in the announcer box. I looked around for Amelia, but she was nowhere to be found.

"Don't worry; she's in a deep sleep. She feels safe with you. She won't be here tonight," he stated, a relief to my mind.

My hand went to my chest again where the port was removed. "Cholangiocarcinoma. Ain't that a bitch, huh? All the cancer really wants to do is live. Isn't that a strange way to think of it? It really *is* a battle. Is that why people say that? That cancer's a battle?" he questioned thoughtfully.

"Yeah, well, it wins," I said as I folded my arms across my chest.

"She can't know that," he warned. "It's pertinent to the mission. I saw the scans. I'm sorry, Kellen," he said and motioned towards a scanned image of my abdomen hanging on the window of the box. The tumor was a bright spot taking up two-thirds of my remaining liver. It could only be removed once, and they did that, but it found its way back.

"Keep her safe," he told me.

I just nodded, still staring at the monster I could no longer fight.

"Kellen," she murmured, her voice sweet and soft on the pillow next to me. It was now three-thirty a.m., and I needed to get her home before my parents realized she was still here. "How did you die?" she asked.

"It was six months after my cancer diagnosis," I began. "I was doing a pretty harsh round of chemotherapies, and I got pneumonia. I knew I was sick; I had no immune system. I didn't tell my mom. I just wanted this all to be over. I knew I was sick enough for it to kill me, so I just let it get worse and worse until one day my mom couldn't wake me up one morning. I was rushed to the hospital where I coded. I was only dead for a minute but it was apparently long enough to be granted a position in this savior business."

"What kind of cancer was it?"

"It's called Cholangiocarcinoma. It's not very well known, and nothing in particular causes it. It's a cancer of the bile duct, but it presents itself in different areas of the body."

"Presents?"

"My tumor developed in my liver. I had surgery four months ago to remove the portion of it where the tumor was growing. They shrunk it down as much as they possibly could with all of the chemo and radiation and then quickly removed it before it could start to grow again."

"So you only have part of a liver?"

"Yeah, it grows back, but not fully."

"Couldn't they just give you a new liver? Find a donor?"

"No. My cancer isn't a liver cancer, remember? It's a bile duct … so I'm not eligible since the cancer could then pop up somewhere else easily or just take over the new liver."

"Thank goodness that's over, right? I can't believe you're playing soccer after having a chunk of your liver taken out!" She hit me on the arm. I cowered.

"You know what you do when you're given a second chance at life? You live it."

When I told Amelia I was getting my line out, she had assumed it was for a more optimistic reason. I didn't have the heart to tell her it was because I was giving up. Derek swore me to secrecy. He could see how this would all end. I had to trust him to lead me down the right path. Plus, he knew Amelia better than I did and would want to protect her at all costs.

Hopefully, however it played out, she wouldn't have to watch me suffer.

chapter twenty three

amelia

Because we had a day off of school yesterday, Kellen's soccer game was moved to the day of the dance. That's why I ended up sitting huddled on the bleachers next to Anthony watching a tangle of legs and feet "dance" on the field. I'm not going to pretend I knew exactly what was going on, but I did know that they needed to get the ball into the goal. That I could follow.

"You're going to help us decorate after the game, right?" Anthony asked. I cringed. "I have to get ready for the dance." I smiled at him.

"For four hours?" He raised his eyebrows and smiled. "I know you better than that Amelia," he said as he nudged me with his shoulder. "You're not that complicated of a person."

"Well, that's exactly why it'll take so long! The hell if I know what I'm doing," I proclaimed. I shivered and tucked myself into a ball. "I'm going to the concessions to get some hot chocolate," I announced.

Anthony looked up at me. "You live in Wisconsin, Amelia," he said with mock disappointment.

"So I should be used to the cold? Never."

He smiled and shook his head. "No, you should be smart enough to have worn your jacket."

On my way to the concessions, I passed a group of high school girls wearing only sports bras on their upper torsos, their bellies painted to spell out the school name. Was that actually necessary? If this had been another lifetime, that might have been me, giggling with friends and freezing my ass off for attention.

No. Let's face it.It wouldn't have.

A few guys stopped to comment on the girl's outfits, and I rolled my eyes. Of course. I turned back to the concessions and was greeted by Corbin's smiling face.

"Ah, mi amore!" he proclaimed and held out his arms. I gladly hugged him for warmth and then lingered longer than necessary. He laughed.

"Are you cold, amore?"

"Just a little," I said, my face still pressed into his shirt.

"Here, take my fleece. I was just about to leave; plus I have a little extra insulation on my body," he said as he shrugged

fly

off his jacket. It was far too big on me, but I wrapped it around myself as tightly as I could and thanked him.

"I have to fly, it was nice seeing you, though. Don't worry about when you'll get the shirt back to me," he said as he kissed my forehead and started to quickly walk away.

I threw the hood over my head and continued.

"Hot chocolate please?" I asked when I reached the counter. No one moved to help me, and when I looked around, everyone in the concession stand was staring over toward the game. I turned to follow their gaze, and it was in that split second I realized the field and crowd had gone completely silent.

Silent in my mind or real life? I stepped to the side, and I could see there was a group of people huddled around someone lying on the ground. When I turned back to the concession stand, I could see they were talking to each other, but at that moment there was really no sound at all.

I didn't think; I just took off into a full-fledged run toward the field, dodging spectators who seemed to be immersed in hushed conversation. The world seemed like a blur. It had to be Kellen; why else would sound bleed from my world? Anthony grabbed my arm just as I was about to step onto the field.

"Amelia," he warned.

I must have looked panicked because he turned me to face him and filled me in immediately. "He just hurt his leg or ankle or something. Just got tangled up with Paul. He's okay," he assured

227

me. Even with Anthony's reassurance, my body was shaking uncontrollably.

People surrounding Kellen lifted him up and helped him hobble over to the sidelines where I was standing with Anthony. His left leg was bent at the knee to keep his ankle off of the ground.

"Hang on a second guys," he said as he reached me. "Millie, I wish you didn't have to witness that." He must have seen the fear and panic on my face despite my attempt to hide it.

"Actually, I didn't. I was at the concessions when things grew eerily silent so I ran over to see what was going on."

"Nothing much, just collided with a teammate. I have to go in to get my ankle checked out, though, to make sure nothing is broken," he said.

"I can meet you there," I started, but he was already shaking his head.

"Go home and get ready for the dance. I'll have Anthony meet up with me at the hospital and then I'll meet you at the dance later, okay?"

"You're what? I don't need to go to the dance, Kellen! That's ridiculous!"

"Well, then I'm ridiculous, because I want to go. I'll meet you there. Go home and get all dressed up, and I'll see you later." He smiled and then winced as he attempted to readjust his stance.

Then he winked, and they started toward the ambulance that is regulatory at every major game.

Anthony turned to me. "Don't worry Amelia; he's a tough cookie. You go decorate, and I'll take care of Kellen."

I shot a look at him and he smiled.

"Go home Amelia. I'll text you with an update later, and I'll see you at the dance."

I watched them walk toward the ambulance, and I wasn't quite sure what to do next. It honestly wouldn't take me that long to get ready so I didn't understand why I couldn't go along, but I wasn't going to dwell on it. It was probably Kellen's idea; he probably just really didn't want to inconvenience me or spoil rest of my plans for the day.

I had no other reason to stay for the rest of the game, so I started back to my car. I absentmindedly reached into my coat pocket for my keys, but they weren't there because it wasn't my coat. My hand came back out with a folded letter addressed to Corbin. I stared at it for a second even though I knew it wasn't mine to read, but I found my keys and slipped into my car before opening it up.

Dearest hermano,

There's this song that used to be the soundtrack of my days and nights, Coldplay's "Fix You." I had eventually deleted it off of my phone, but last night it popped up in a YouTube playlist as I stood in the kitchen making dinner.

I stopped and stared at the screen for the whole time it played, absorbing all the emotion it expressed.

At this time in 2003, I was learning that Luis had died. Remember when I dated him? He took one too many pain pills on accident and just never woke up.

I was at the bar that night, a Thursday night after bowling league, with Mom and Dad, and I was coming home because you wanted to have a fire with friends, and Mom and Dad required an adult to be there. I was coming home for you. Because we were friends. And I would do something like that for you.

As I was walking out of PJs and getting into dad's truck, I got the call. He was driving through the parking lot, not yet to Edgewood. I actually tried to get out of the truck as it was moving because I was so confused.

Death does that. Shuts you down. Makes the world stop and spin at the same time. When I got home, I was only in the kitchen a few steps before my knees gave way, and I buckled to the ground in sobs. Dad had to eventually help me to my feet, and I spent the next few hours sitting on the floor in front of my bed staring at my dresser.

Luis's memory followed me for years after that. He was who I compared everyone to. That day haunted me, and it still does in many ways.

Last year on this day, I didn't have time to let that memory replay in my head. I spent the whole day talking with mom and whoever else about your impending intervention. I spent the whole day not knowing what would happen. Possibilities ranged from death (of anyone) to some sort of hope that things might be successful.

My career, my position as an AODA counselor, was like going overseas and being the nurse in a war from which most people never return. The kind about which people say, "It's bad there," but no one really ever understands fully what that means until the person has been there. And if they had been there ... well then you see their face turn to pained horror because they know you've signed a death sentence unless granted a miracle.

So that night, when I walked into the house, I barely blinked when I walked over the exact spot in which I had previously fallen. The bedroom in which I sat in the dark was not my own, and this time I was joined by Dad (and eventually Mom) and I tried to tell them stories and bring them ease as we waited for you.

I absorbed that moment because I wasn't sure what would come 'after.' That was our last normal moment. And I have every whisper and laugh and moment of unease stored away in my memory.

I deleted the song from my phone in June. When I was struggling to remember who I was because I got so lost in everything going on around me. When I came to realize what the end of your war would look like and that I didn't know how to fix it. When no one had the capability to listen to someone who knew what the other side looked like. When I failed to remember that we had ever been friends.

The song no longer applies because I'm not struggling on a daily basis to 'fix' anything. Nothing can be 'fixed' ... not by my hand anyway. Not even me, though I'm honestly working on that.

Instead the chorus starting at 3:30 reaches deep into everything I am and feel, and it shakes my very core because I still feel sometimes like I'm standing in this massive rubble. Instead of asking how to get out, the only question I can manage is, "How did we even get here?"

I hope you win your war, Corbin.

After I finished reading the note, I immediately grabbed my cell phone and dialed Corbin's number. It rang four times before he answered.

"Amelia, *mi amore*," he answered in a partly slurred voice.

"Hey, Corbin. Where are you?" I tried to stay calm.

"I'm just waiting," he said softly. "I'm glad you called. I'm glad you'll be the one."

"The one what? What's going on, Corbin?"

"I just ..." He trailed off.

"Corbin," I said sternly.

"Yeah?"

"You just what?'

232

"Oh. It's okay; I'm okay now. I just caused so much pain, you know?"

"Are you talking about the letter from your sister?" I asked. "I read it Corbin. It was in your coat. I'm worried about you. Tell me what's going on."

"I tried, for so long, you know?"

"No, I don't know. What are you talking about?"

"I got the pills ... when I hurt myself a few years ago."

"The pills?"

"Yeah, pain pills. I took them as prescribed ... but then when it was over I just ... I still needed them, you know? I needed them to stay calm. Every time I tried to stop; I was in pain and bursting with anxiety. So I found more. I couldn't stop. I can't stop. It's almost over ..." His voice started to trail at the end, getting softer and softer as though he were falling asleep.

"What's almost over? Corbin, where are you? Tell me where you are," I demanded. I stepped out of my car and looked back at the crowd of people at the field. I needed someone else's phone. I needed to call Corbin's house. I needed to find out where he was.

"Cor," I started, "tell me about your family."

"I let them down, Amelia. They'll never forgive me. They kicked me out last night. After they found out I stole money from their dresser drawer. I didn't mean to. I just, I didn't have any other options, you know? It's like I'm two different people. One who wants to get better and the other who can only live with the pills. I can't be two different people anymore, Amelia. It's exhausting. I'm exhausted."

"Corbin, they love you. They'll always love you."

I reached a group of people, and I put my phone on mute. "I need a phone. Now!" I demanded. No one questioned me, and someone handed over her iPhone. I quickly pulled up the browser and searched for his parents to try to get a phone number. I knew what street he lived on, so I could only make an assumption about who they were. As soon as a number popped up, I hit dial. I switched back to Corbin and asked him another question to keep him talking so he wouldn't notice I wasn't talking.

His dad answered on the first ring, and I quickly explained that I thought something was wrong and we needed to figure out where Corbin was immediately.

"I know where he goes. I know where he might be," he said, and I heard him start up his car. He was on a landline so the phone started to crackle with static. "Keep him on the phone and come to the house," he said right before the phone cut out.

I quickly handed the phone back to whomever had handed it to me and started running towards my car.

"Corbin?" I asked.

"I'm tired, Em," he said in a low hush.

Corbin's dad was right in his assumption about where he would be and luckily had an ambulance en route before he could

fly

confirm his supposition. Corbin had taken enough pain pills to kill himself, despite his tolerance. He coded on the way to the hospital, but luckily the paramedics carried Narcan and were able to bring him back to life. He was asking for me at the hospital, so I was on my way there, stopping quickly at a gas station. I was pumping my gas when I heard someone say my name just a few inches from my face. I turned to see Paul standing next to me. I must have been so deep in thought that I hadn't heard him approach.

"I'm so sorry, Amelia," he said. "It was an accident, I swear."

My furrowed brow must have given away my confusion and the fact I was not thinking clearly after everything that had just transpired, so he went on. "About Kellen. His ankle?"

"Oh. Why? I mean, why are you sorry?" I asked.

"Well, I was the one who got tangled up with him," he said as though he expected me to know.

"Accidents happen Paul; he'll be fine," I assured him.

"Well, let me make it up to you. Let me take you to the dance tonight on his behalf," he said.

A shiver ran down my spine, and the gas pump clicked to indicate t my tank was full. I glanced over at him, my skin still crawling. "Oh, Kellen is still going to the dance. Thank you though; that was thoughtful. Hey, I'm sorry, but I'm in a hurry. I really have to get going."

fly

I hurriedly jumped into my car. I stared at the steering wheel for a moment before turning the engine on. The feeling of 'get the hell out of here' came out of nowhere. I could say with certainty my mission was for Corbin … but why didn't it feel like it was over?

chapter twenty four

I reached the dance not long after it had begun. I had to write a police report once I arrived at the hospital and then I spent a while talking to Corbin's dad who did nothing but praise me for thinking fast on my feet. I wanted to tell him I did nothing out of the ordinary, but I knew that was not what he wanted to hear, so I thanked him for his kind words instead.

Corbin was being seen by all types of doctors, so I didn't get much time to talk to him, but he let me know I did the right thing and he was glad that he was getting help.

I filled Kellen in with the brief version over the phone on my way to the dance. The dance that he somehow beat me to.

When I walked up to the school entrance, Anthony was waiting for me by the door. "Your boyfriend is a gimp, so he sent me out to get you. Something about needing to save all of his energy so he can hobble around the dance floor with you and probably look like a huge idiot," Anthony told me.

I gave him a look.

"Well, I obviously added the idiot part," he said. "But seriously Amelia, look at you!" He stopped and turned me toward him. "You clean up nice, kid! Do me a favor and plant a wet one on my cheek and be sure to smear some lipstick on there. Makes me look more desirable to the ladies." He pointed to his cheek.

"I'm not wearing any lipstick, doofus. Let's go. I want to see Kellen."

When I walked into the seating area, the voices were suddenly overwhelming. It wasn't just loud or that it was a big group of people, but I could hear *everything*. Not just voices, but all of the conversations at once. Not just music, but the DJ thumbing through some CDs.

"Millie?" I heard Kellen ask, but I just glanced toward him in hurried confusion. The sound was taking over my ability to process any thoughts. I stared at him blankly. He handed one crutch to Anthony and grabbed my hand with the other, pulling me out into the hallway.

"Amelia." He cradled my face in his hands and stepped toward me. The hallway clock was ticking loudly, and the couple that was down the hall from us was having a fight. A door opening sounded like an explosion in my head. I stared into Kellen's eyes, and he must have seen how much I was struggling because he asked me to dance.

"I can't go back in there," I told him.

"Then we'll dance out here," he said. He pulled out his cell phone, turned on a soft song and started to sway back and forth the best he could on one foot. He still leaned on one crutch. It was awkward, but we made it work.

"Is this helping?" he asked.

I nodded, but when he looked me in the eyes he knew it wasn't. He stared down at me for a beat and then pulled my head to rest on his chest. He took his free hand and covered my ear as we continued to slowly sway.

Thump, thump, thump.

Just like that, the rhythm of his heartbeat was the only sound I could hear, and my mind went completely blank.

Thump, thump, thump.

"Amelia," I heard my name in a whisper.

I pulled away from him, and the silence was still there.

"Hmm?" I responded still in a trance.

A phone started to ring, and I stepped to Kellen's side to look in the direction of the sound.

Now the phone was the only sound I heard, and it was coming from the men's restroom down the hall.

chapter twenty five

As the men's door swung open, all the sound came crashing back to me and Paul emerged. Except it was not a cell phone he was holding; it was a gun, and in that moment I was unable to move. He smiled as he stepped toward us.

"I honestly didn't think it'd be this easy," he said as he raised the gun.

"Paul, what are you doing?" Kellen asked.

"Look, Kellen, I'm sorry. I don't have time to chat." His eyes were cold, his face emotionless. "I just have to do this one thing, and I'm cleared of my debts to Adam," he said. "Sorry Amelia, this would have been easier had you just agreed to go to the dance with me. I could have picked you up at your house, and we wouldn't have had this awkward dance of the why and the what. Kellen here," he pointed his weapon at Kellen, "he had to be all macho and continue to come to this stupid place despite his injury. My mistake."

Anthony told me he got tangled up with Paul.

It wasn't an accident.

What the hell was going on?

I heard someone laughing in the distance, and when they rounded the corner to see us, their laughter turned into screams as they ran the other way. Why couldn't I run? I wanted to run. I couldn't leave Kellen here.

"Time's up," he said as he motioned the gun back at me and fired it.

chapter twenty six
kellen

She was lying on the ground, not moving.

My beautiful Millie.

I tried so hard over the last few weeks to find something about her that bothered me because I knew there had to be *something,* but all I could do was fall more and more in love with her.

There was a puddle of blood spreading beneath her.

My heart was breaking into a million pieces, but they weren't mine; those pieces belonged to her.

I wanted to give them to her. I wanted to make her stronger, more resilient.

I wanted her to thrive in this life. To make the most of it, get the best out of it.

I wished I could breathe her in at that moment. I wished I could rest my head beneath her jawline as she lay there and just rest my head on her chest to listen to her heartbeat like she did mine.

What did it feel like when your heart shattered?

Right then it felt like a car was resting on my chest.

I couldn't breathe.

I stared at her face, memorizing her one more time.

Was the last thing you saw before you died forever engraved at the forefront of your mind?

I wished I could see her beautiful eyes, see into her soul one last time.

I wished for that, but I was also grateful she wouldn't have to see this.

It was then that I took my last breath.

chapter twenty seven

amelia

Kellen was pronounced dead on arrival at the hospital. The pronouncement would have happened at the scene, but the EMTs weren't allowed to do that, and they wanted to try to do anything they could to save him.

But they couldn't.

It was too late.

The night was a whirlwind of events, but the last thing I remembered was getting hit hard on my right side and then hitting the wall beside me. I awoke drenched in a puddle of blood, but it wasn't my own. I thought I had died. Now I wished I had. I was lying in my bed, motionless, and staring at the wall. I had this brief moment when I woke up from an exhaustion-induced sleep when I thought it wasn't real. Then it all came flooding back to me, and I felt like I was breaking all over again. The scenes flashed through my mind like a horror movie. The feel and smell of the blood that took forever to wash from my skin, the screams and sobs from the people surrounding us after Paul had fled, the sirens blaring as they carried me out to the ambulance unsure if I was hurt or not. I couldn't cry. I could only stare forward.

My phone started to vibrate, and I glanced down to see Anthony's name pop up on the screen.

I didn't want to talk to anyone now, but I was willing to listen. I hit the answer button and transferred it to speaker. I tried to say hello, but when I opened my mouth nothing came out. He knew I was there, so he just started talking.

"Amelia. I don't even know what to say to you right now. I just …" he trailed off. "I needed to call you. I knew you wouldn't want to hear from anyone, but he had some things he wanted me to tell you if anything ever happened to him."

At this, I reflexively sat up on my bed and grabbed my phone as though I only had one chance to hear whatever it was he had to say.

He cleared his throat and continued. "He was sick, Amelia. His cancer was back, and there was nothing else they could do. He had the port taken out simply because he didn't need any more treatments. He didn't want you to know because he wanted to spend his days watching you smile and laugh instead of watching him as if every move could possibly be his last. He told me so when we went to get his ankle checked out after the game. I thought he was telling me this because he wanted me to tell you down the road in case anything happened. He couldn't have known …"

My sobs became heavy again, and my body ached in harmony with the gut-wrenching sound that was coming from my soul.

"Amelia," he said softly. "There's a note on your dresser from him. You were sleeping, so I didn't want to disturb you, and I just left it there. He also told me to tell you something. He wanted me to use his exact words, so hang on a second while I pull up his text." He sounded distant now because his face was further from the phone. "He said to tell you his mission was to save you."

I froze.

"Call me if you need me, okay? Even if it's to use me as a punching bag, just call me. I love you."

The screen flashed before my home screen appeared signifying that the call had ended. I quickly got up and grabbed the envelope off my dresser. At the sight of his handwriting on the envelope I started to cry.

My beautiful Millie,

I'm sorry.

I'm sorry I have to write this to you. But if you're reading it, you're alive.

That's all that really matters.

Last night I visited Derek, and he handed me a sheet of paper and asked me to tell you goodbye. How do I even do that? I may have only known you a short while, but to me it felt like an entire lifetime while at the same time it felt like not long enough.

Time.

Thanks to the cancer, I didn't have much left, Millie. I wanted all of my days to be filled with memories of you.

They weren't enough. I wanted a lifetime with you. I needed a lifetime with you.

I was never grateful for living until I met you. It was the first time I was grateful that I was brought back to life. It was the first time I felt like I could breathe in a world that only seemed to be suffocating me.

I saved you, Amelia.

I saved you so you could live.

People are going to bombard you with all of those bullshit sayings about how I'm in a better place, and I'm not suffering anymore, and the sun always rises, and whatever else they can come up with. Let it roll off of your shoulders. My place was with you, but for whatever reason, I can't stay.

Do the only thing you can do with this life and make it matter.

Whatever it was that made you cry that night, it didn't 'happen for a reason' like some people try to tell a person when something bad happens. It didn't. There's never a reason to be hurt like you were. But you can take it and make it into something that matters. Do good with your pain. If you can do anything for me, do that.

If I'm lucky enough, maybe I'll get to see you in your dreams. I'm not really sure how that whole thing works. If I can't, I just want to leave you with a bit of Kellen advice. It's again inspired by that poem I told you about; the one that essentially says when you think you're out of options, there's always one more.

Overcome it. Whatever it is. Do it for me.

When you're backed to the edge of a cliff, don't fall Millie, fly.

I love you, Amelia. Always.

Kellen

epilogue

The days following Kellen's death I didn't sleep. My grandmother took me to the doctor and I went home with a trial pack of sleeping pills to help me through the first week. I normally wouldn't take any medication because of my attempted suicide, but I was desperate. I took a pill when we got home from the doctor even though it was only 4 p.m. I didn't want to be awake anymore.

That's when it first happened.

I opened my eyes in a dream state, and I was sitting on a beach watching the waves lap on the shore. It was warm and quiet with the exception of the water. I sat and took it all in for a few minutes before curling into a ball and breaking down into a sobbing mess. I felt someone sit down next to me but I was too embarrassed to look up.

"Millie …"

I froze. Everything inside of me turned to stone and I held my breath afraid to move. I felt him get up from beside me and reposition his body behind mine. He settled his legs on either side of me and pulled me back to rest against his chest.

Thump, thump. Thump, thump. His heart echoed into my ear.

acknowledgments

This book started out years ago as a writing challenge to keep myself busy. With encouragement from many people I pulled it out from time to time to work on it and hoped to one day say it was finished. I never would have met that goal if it weren't for many people. From the bottom of my heart, thank you:

To my mom who relentlessly pushed me to finish and publish this book. Without her it would probably continue to be in limbo. Thank you for your support and for believing in me. Above all, thank you for being proud of me.

To my dad. You made this book possible in so many ways that you will never know. I heard you loud and clear with every person who walked through your funeral line and told me to write a book.

To all of my early beta readers with special thanks to Anthony Laatsch, Michelle Stephan and Alesia Kritz. Your excitement and encouragement kept me going.

To my loving husband Kevin. Your text messages asking for the next chapter (long before we even dated) made me excited to be writing. Thank you for believing in me early on and thank you for making sure this dream came true. I love you.

To Jennifer Loya for being my first ever fan and always believing in me. I love you.

To Jess Gerek for encouraging me to be proud to be who I am.

To Stephanie Lockwood for being the first person to thoroughly read my book. Your daily emails and texts of excitement for my book meant more to me than you can know.

To my beautiful Ruthie for creating the cover art and Shannon Kozlowicz of Red Ribbon Editing for bringing life to my cover through my vision.

To my editor, Carmen Comeaux, for being so kind, patient, and encouraging. Sometimes I wanted to give up but you made me feel like my book was worth it.

To Sara Mack and Red Ribbon Editing for all the work you did helping this dream become a reality. Thank you for your kindness, encouragement and for holding my hand through this whole process. I wouldn't have been able to do this without your help ;)

And lastly, but most important, to my daughter Celia and son Emmett for making me want to be the best version of myself I can be. You are my world and I hope you always find a way to fly.

about the author

Erica Monzingo grew up in Wisconsin where she currently resides with her husband, daughter and son. She graduated with a degree in AODA Counseling but is currently taking time off to raise her children. If there is one thing that has never changed it is that she is never without a book and has always had a great appreciation for story telling through any form. Her spare time is spent blogging about life experiences, listening to NPR, and drinking coffee.

You can find Erica on Facebook at:
https://www.facebook.com/authorericamonzingo

Made in the USA
San Bernardino, CA
28 December 2016